Real Vampires
Take a Bite Out of Christmas

GERRY BARTLETT

REAL VAMPIRES TAKE A BITE OUT OF CHRISTMAS

Copyright © 2014 Gerry Bartlett

Dragon Lady Publishing. League City, Texas, USA

ISBN-13: 978-0991486052
ISBN: 0991486056

DEDICATION

To the **Real Vampires Fan Group** on Facebook
You guys are a wonderful support!
Thanks for always being there.

.

ONE

I had a knot the size of Austin in the pit of my stomach. Stupid. So I'd finally said "yes" to my long-time lover. I wore his ring, a five-carat beauty that felt heavy and strange on my finger. Not a shackle, a commitment. Which I was ready for. Seriously. Just seeing Jeremiah Campbell's happy smile as he directed workmen to tear down walls in my apartment convinced me I'd done the right thing. I wrapped my arms around his waist.

"Big project you've got going on here. You sure all this is necessary?" I leaned against him.

"You'll love it. Master bedroom adequate enough for my king-sized bed, a bath with a soaking tub and those jets you like; not to mention a walk-in shower that will fit both of us comfortably." He turned to hold me against him. His dark eyes reminded me of wild times in dozens of showers. The man did know his way around a tile enclosure. "Want me to tell the workers to knock off for the night? Let me give you a personal tour?"

"Tempting." I briefly kissed his firm lips then lingered. These mortal workmen didn't have a clue they were in an apartment with two vampires. Jerry's fangs slid down and I played with them for a moment before I pulled back. "Later. The sooner this project is done, the sooner we can move in and start our new life together."

"About that life. Gloriana St. Clair, you've been dodging my questions lately. How about some answers?" He led me out into the hall. I'd lived in 2B.

We carefully avoided two men carrying a piece of granite up the stairs and into unit 2A where Lacy, a werecat and the day manager for my shop downstairs, had lived until recently. Jerry had bought the entire building for us and was turning this floor into our apartment. Lacy had taken being evicted surprisingly well and had found other living arrangements. I hadn't had a chance yet to ask her what those were. Jerry's hand stroking my butt brought me back to the problem at hand.

Questions. At first I hadn't thought past saying yes to his proposal. Being practical, Jer had immediately bombarded me with those questions about how and where we'd live, the inevitable changes to our relationship, and any number of things that had made me scared to commit. Of course he wanted answers. But would he like what I had to say? The knot in my stomach was now the size of the entire Lone Star State.

"Okay, let's get this over with. I've been thinking. You're a traditional man, Jeremiah Campbell or

Jeremy Blade, whatever name you wish to use when we marry. I've become a modern woman." I ran my hands over his chest. I did love those hard muscles. My guy had been a Highland warrior hundreds of years ago and had the scars to prove it. He would always have the look--keen eyes and a sturdy frame that dared anyone to take him on. I knew that even now he could lay his hand on a number of weapons if a threat appeared.

My stubborn, handsome, invincible Scot. He'd faced danger many times. For me, for the people he loved. I adored that about him. I felt fiercely protective of him too and would risk everything to keep him from getting hurt. I let him see that in my eyes and he pulled me tight against him.

"Ah, Gloriana, my love. I know you've changed. I loved you then and I love you now. Please trust me to deal with whatever you have on your mind." He ran his hands up and down my back. I'd seen him do it before when calming a fractious horse. Yep, that was me. The fractious part anyway. Thinking of bolting.

I took a breath. Okay, so it worked. I was settling down. "First, I'd like to keep my name. Stay Gloriana St. Clair. I have a business that I plan to continue running, a Facebook presence, lots of connections who know me by that name. So I won't become Mrs. Campbell. Definitely not Mrs. Blade." I smiled to take the sting out of that. "Hey, I don't carry knives everywhere like you do." I slid a hand under the back of his shirt and plucked out a dagger to prove my point.

"Careful, that's sharp." He had it settled into its custom sheath before one of the workmen could see it. Then he firmed his lips, thinking about the name thing. I knew he wasn't thrilled. It was how in the primitive part of him thought to claim me.

"Gloriana…"

"Hear me out, Jer. Your mother hates me anyway. She'll be over the moon that I'm not sullying the great Campbell name."

"Like I care what she thinks." He scanned the room and frowned. "Come with me." He dragged me down the hall, to yet another vacant apartment. It made me wonder just how big our new place was going to be. He'd kept some of the details as a "surprise." He opened a door and pushed me inside then shut us in, flipping the lock. I glanced around. Most of the walls were down in here too. I started to ask about it but he put a finger over my lips. "Listen to me."

I stiffened. I hated taking orders. But this was obviously important so I just stared up at him.

"You would do the Campbell name proud. If you ever, ever say again that you're not good enough for me, I swear I'll put you over my knee and beat the daylights out of you." His hands tightened on my shoulders. He was deadly serious. It was sweet and a little scary.

"You've never hit me before, Jerry. And I know I've provoked you." I looked up at him through my lashes. "Beat me? On my bare bottom?" I slid my hand down to tease the bulge in his jeans. As usual, my man was quick to respond. "I haven't seen daylight in over four hundred years. How hard would you have to spank to get the daylights out of me?" I slid down his zipper. He was hot and hard, going commando, my fascinating lover.

"Are you saying you need a good spanking, my love?" He growled, his fangs down and his eyes narrow.

"It would be something new to try. I've been reading some interesting books lately. It seems that, for some people, it can be quite a turn-on." I stroked his erection, rubbing my thumb over the moisture at the tip. "But then you didn't want to excite me, you wanted to punish me. For thinking that an actress, a lowly commoner, might not be good enough for the heir to Clan Campbell." I sighed when he grasped the edge of my sweater and pulled it up and then tossed it out of the way, He proved once again that he had excellent fine motor skills, popping open the front clasp of my bra with one hand while he pushed his other hand into the back of my spandex jeans. I do love pants that stretch.

"This is just one reason I love you, Gloriana St. Clair. You have never failed to surprise me. Just when I think we might begin to fall into a pattern, you turn the tables, invent something new."

"A pattern? Why that sounds way too much like boredom." I continued to play with his cock and walked us back toward a rough table had been made out of a piece of plywood laid across a pair of sawhorses. It was set up next to where a kitchen was being torn apart. Various utensils were scattered on the countertop. "If I ever bore you, promise to file for divorce."

"Bore me? I don't think that will be a problem." Jerry stopped when I grabbed a rubber spatula and thrust it into his hand. "What's this for?"

I shoved my jeans and panties down to my knees and leaned over the table, offering him my bare bottom. "Figure it out, Jer. I think I've been a bad, bad girl. Your mother was right. I was never good enough for you. It's a mistake for you to marry me. I bet you haven't even told her our news yet. You surely won't invite your parents to the wedding, will you?"

"That's enough, Gloriana."

"No, I can see it now. When the priest asks if there is anyone with a reason why this couple should not marry, your mother will rush the altar and beg you to come to your senses." I rested my head on my folded arms and closed my eyes. Would he do it? Abusing women wasn't in Jer's wheelhouse. But this was a game. And— I felt the sting of the rubber hitting my ass. It wasn't a love tap.

"Ow!"

"Our marriage isn't a joke. I called my folks as soon as you agreed to marry me. Mum's first question was if we'd set a date."

"Probably so she could figure out if she had time to talk you out of it." Whap.

"I'll not have you talking like that. I don't give a damn if my parents approve or not, Gloriana. You are *my* choice. Da made it clear they would be at the wedding and greet you happily as the newest member of the family."

"Now you're making me dread my own wedding day." I sighed and rubbed my bum. "This isn't as exciting as the books make it out to be. Have you had enough?"

"Not yet." The spatula whispered across my tender flesh and I quickly moved my hands out of the way. Now this was more like it. The gentle brush of plastic between my buttocks could definitely be a turn-on.

"Okay, keep going then." I kept my eyes closed, enjoying the feeling as he ran his hand across what I was sure were bright pink cheeks back there.

"Set a date. You keep putting me off. I need for you to name the day for our wedding." The spatula tapped me one, two, three times. Gentle blows.

I owed him answers. I braced myself. "June. A June wedding." That earned me a serious swat.

"You're mad. No fucking way I'm waiting until June."

"It's a traditional month. And I want to do it up right." I was sure he'd lose it now. Jerry rarely cursed in front of me. Not the "f" word anyway. So that meant I'd pissed him off. I forced myself to lie still. If he beat me until my bum was a bloody mess, we'd end up drinking from each other anyway. The scent of fresh blood is such a turn-on for vampires. I waited, scared and maybe a little excited. But instead of another hit, I felt Jerry's lips on my stinging flesh. I moaned when his tongue licked away the pain of his punishment.

"Are you sure you want to wait that long?" He turned me over and watched me, waiting.

How could I disappoint a man who seemed to know my heart better than I knew it myself? "It's just a ceremony, Jer. A formality." He picked up the spatula. "Wait! I know it means a lot to you. And you've been very patient with me. Truly." I reached up to rub his cheek. His frown made me want to cry. I had to fix this.

He threw the spatula away. "Then why do you keep putting me off? Are you sure this delay isn't because you still have feelings for Valdez? Or Caine?"

"Jerry! No. They're my friends. That's all." I pulled up my jeans, wincing when the fabric hit my tender tush. Rafael Valdez had been my bodyguard and we'd had an affair. But that had been over long ago. Israel Caine, famous rock star and my one-time fantasy man, had been a one-night stand when Jerry had gone home to Scotland and left me on my own. I know, not an excuse. Since then I'd accepted that Jerry was the one and only man for me. But Rafe and Ray were still in my life and Jerry was jealous of both of them. I didn't blame him. I sure didn't like seeing his old lovers around *him*. But I had to erase his doubts.

"I'm ready to marry you. I am." I knew this was one time that distracting him with sex was the wrong move. I bit my lip. He just stood there, staring at me. Waiting.

"Are you? Then prove it. If they are no longer competition for me, then you won't mind setting a date, a date not that far away, and then announcing it to them and the world."

I took a breath. Put up or shut up. It was only fair. "Fine. I don't have a problem with that. Are you okay with me keeping my name?" I noticed that he'd zipped up his jeans so I pulled my bra back together. No more lovemaking tonight. Too bad.

"If it's that important to you. But you'll wear my rings. I want everyone to know you're taken." He stopped me when I grabbed my sweater. "Don't cover up. I like to look at you." He picked up the spatula again. "Did this do it for you? Turn you on?"

I pulled it out of his hand. "No!" I broke it in half and tossed it into the sink. "Pain doesn't work for me and I hope you don't want me to--"

"Beat me with something?" He grinned and jerked off his shirt, throwing it on the table. "No, thanks. But you can bite me, anywhere, any time."

I nipped at his shoulder. "Good to know."

"You're beautiful, Gloriana. Is your bum still sore?"

"A little." I smiled. "Want to kiss it again and make it better?"

"Why not? I'll get there. Eventually." He efficiently got rid of my bra then leaned down and sucked one nipple into his mouth.

I moaned and grasped his hair. He did know exactly how to please me. When one of his fangs drew blood, my own fangs came down. Oh, yes. We would drink from each other tonight and make slow, delicious love. But first I had something I needed to say.

"Jerry, look at me."

He raised his head, licking a drop of my blood from his lips. "What is it?"

"New Year's Day. What do you think? Wouldn't that be the perfect time for us to start our new life together?" I brushed his hair back from his face. I loved him so much my heart squeezed. Why had I been so reluctant to commit to this man?

"You want our wedding day on New Year's Day?" His smile twisted my heart even more. It took so little to make him happy.

"It won't be easy. We're busy in the shop before Christmas, but--"

"No, I'll take it. That gives me a month. If I pay overtime I can have our apartment ready by then." He kissed me hard and deep. "I love you, Gloriana. Never doubt it. I can't wait to start the New Year

9

with you as my wife." He slid down my zipper again. "I think this calls for a celebration."

"Yes, it does." I helped him work off my snug jeans and kicked my heels across the room. In moments we were both naked. "I'm worried now. Patterns. We need to keep things fresh between us, Jer."

He laughed. "You want fresh? Gloriana, I have had you many, many ways in hundreds of places. What do you suggest?"

I glanced around, suddenly out of ideas. There wasn't much to work with here and standing in front of him naked under the harsh overhead lights didn't suit me. He might notice the imperfections I dressed carefully to disguise. I had a generous figure, especially in the hip area. I'd just about decided to pick up the plywood and hold it in front of me when he dragged me against him.

"Relax, sweetheart. Do we always have to reinvent the wheel?" He chuckled and kissed my hair.

"I should read more, watch porn or something. And lovemaking is an important part of our relationship, Jer." I said this to his chest, distracted by the yummy masculine smell of him. He was clean and I could hear the blood throbbing through his veins.

"We don't need porn or a manual to enjoy each other. But there's something I'd like from you." He leaned back and stared into my eyes. "Will you sing to me? I was blown away when I finally heard you sing on Halloween. After all those centuries, to get your Siren's voice back... It's a bloody miracle, isn't it?" He smoothed his hand over my throat. " Ever since that night, I've been imagining you singing to me while I make you come."

"Jeremiah Campbell!" Shocking but then I had to admit I liked the idea. Now that I could sing without sounding like a goat giving birth to a rhino, I did at every opportunity. I couldn't wait to sing in that double shower he was building for us. "Any special requests?"

"Surprise me." He pulled me down to a pile of cotton drop clothes in the corner of the former living room. When his mouth landed on my stomach and began working its way down, I began singing a very wobbly version of "Have Yourself a Merry Little Christmas." I felt him smile against my skin.

"Like that one?"

"Yes, and I plan to have a very merry time indeed." He spread my legs and pulled them up over his shoulders. "What have we here? An early present. Don't quit singing now. No matter what happens."

"Troubles out of..." I couldn't seem to remember the words as his tongue played with the spot that he knew drove me wild. My hips bucked off the floor and he gentled me again, this time with a soothing hand on my breast. I held onto his hair, that thick so wonderfully soft hair that would always be dark and never streak with gray.

"Sing, love. I think there's something about 'golden days' coming up." He glanced up, pushing his finger inside me while he raised my hips even more. "Your blood is pounding in your veins, keeping time."

"Faithful friends," my voice rose so high I feared for the glass in the windows. His fangs pierced my vein, there in my upper thigh. He'd hit the sweet spot and the pull of his mouth along with his fingers inside me sent me tumbling over the edge into ecstasy. I shivered, trembled, and pressed my legs together so hard he had to pry them apart.

"Careful, Gloriana, you've almost cracked my skull." He'd licked the punctures closed and grinned up at me before he slid up my body and pushed his cock inside my still quivering center. I screamed, sure the workmen would come running to see who was being murdered.

"If the fates allow, Jer, I do hope we'll always be together." I pulled his head down to kiss him, licking my way into his mouth and holding him as if I'd never let him go. I sang to him in my mind, verse after verse, until we were both relaxed and satisfied in each other's arms.

"A merry Christmas it will be." Jerry stretched then stood. "Let me show you around the place, explain exactly what the men are doing here. We can plan where to put the Christmas tree and hang the mistletoe. If you see anything you don't like, I'll change the plans." He helped me up then began to pull on his clothes.

I watched him, sure that no other man would ever make me feel the way this one did. He cherished me, pampered me and put up with my faults and had for over four hundred years.

"I love you, Jeremiah Campbell." I ran into his arms, suddenly overcome with the need to hold him again.

"Why, Gloriana, is there something wrong? You seem a little upset." He held me close, brushing my hair back from my face. "Am I being too controlling, taking over the apartment planning? I know you hate it when I ignore your wishes."

"No, no! You've been wonderful. You're more

than I deserve." Stupid tears. Where had they come from? He loved me and he'd proved it over and over again. So why did I feel like he'd come to his senses any moment now? It was a good thing I'd named a date only a month away. He'd have no time to examine our relationship and run away screaming from his near miss.

"There you go again. Where is that damned kitchen utensil?" He popped my butt with his bare hand. "Maybe you did get off to the hitting then. Since you seem determined to provoke me." He lifted my chin. "You are the only woman I want. The only woman I am willing to spend eternity with. Are you clear on that?"

"Yes." I blinked and, instead of a blur, his handsome face came into focus. "I'll try to get over this insecurity. But I've had it a long, long time. And I come with baggage. A mother who is a goddess from Olympus."

"Some men would think that's a bonus. She gave you some fine skills, didn't she?"

"Hah! She'll be the mother-in-law from hell, mark my words." I rubbed his cheek, a little rough from his evening beard, with my thumb. "I'm warning you, Jer. She's going to be trouble. Worse than your mother will be."

"I can handle her." He smiled and ran his hand down my back. "At least she hasn't produced a father for you yet. That could a real problem. He might not like the fact that I've taken over four hundred years to make an honest woman of you."

"I've always been an honest woman." I slipped away from him and began pulling on my clothes. "I don't need a wedding ring to prove that."

"Here we go. And just when I thought we'd reached a fine understanding." Jerry waited until I was fully dressed then unlocked the door. "Is it safe to open this?"

"Sure. Let the workers see who was screeching her pleasure a few minutes ago. No embarrassment here." I rolled my eyes then strutted out the door. Jerry grabbed me around the waist and jerked me to him.

"Never be embarrassed to be a passionate woman, Gloriana. And my woman at that." He kissed my lips, catching me trying to bite back a grin.

"Easy for you to say. You want them to think you're a stud who makes your 'woman' scream every time you do her." I popped him on his taut butt. "Arrogant ass."

He laughed, his eyes bright. He looked more relaxed than I'd seen him in a long, long time. It made me want to pull him back into that room and go another round. Make *him* scream.

"Vixen. Come, look over this place and tell me what to make bigger and what to change."

I looked down at his zipper. "There are some things that could always be bigger. But I'll let that go." I squealed when he pinched my butt. "Don't change a thing, Jer. Not a thing."

Laughing we began our tour. I linked arms with him, flushing every time I caught a worker giving me the eye. So this was what it felt like to be happy. Could it last? I didn't dare start analyzing it. Right now I planned to just live in the moment, my biggest worry that I had a mere month to plan the wedding I'd always dreamed of. I needed reinforcements and I knew just who to call.

TWO

"It is impossible. The wedding of your dreams in a month?" My best friend, Florence Da Vinci, threw up her hands. "You don't even have a dress."

"I know. It'll be a challenge too. I won't wear white. Makes me look fat." Of course Flo glowed in that color. Tonight she wore winter white head to toe. I'd have looked like a giant snowball in her bulky sweater, and there was no way I'd ever cram my thighs into a pair of skinny jeans.

"You are *not* fat. You have generous curves. Eh?" Flo stomped around my vintage clothing shop, muttering in Italian.

"Thanks. I like to see it that way. Luckily, the man in my life is ancient and likes a full figure." I didn't need to understand the language to know Flo hated everything in here. We had agreed to disagree a long time ago. I loved to give old clothes a new home.

She liked everything that touched her body to be brand new when she bought it.

She stopped her Italian tirade and faced me, hands on hips that were a tiny size six. "I hope you're not planning to wear a used wedding dress. No, I won't allow it. We must buy you something wonderful and *new*. My treat. A wedding present."

"No, that's too much. Besides, I like vintage. I'm sure I can find--"

She cut me off with a gesture. "I will. Don't make me fight with you. We have no time for this." She obviously considered the matter settled. "Now, moving on. Something borrowed, something blue. I loan you some diamond earrings. Or maybe a necklace and you wear the sapphires I gave you for the blue."

Oh, yes. The earrings had been my "engagement" present. She was generous, a great friend, but I was beginning to feel like Flo's favorite charity case. My good jewelry consisted of the ring on my finger, those earrings she'd given me and a fake Rolex that needed a new battery. When she started in on my underwear, I became determined to stop Flo's monologue. I was *not* poor, damn it. I could buy my own freaking thong.

"No, say nothing. I can see you are going to make me unhappy." She wagged a finger in my face. "I can and will buy your dress." Her eyes glistened as she grabbed my shoulders. "Look at me. I do this. For our friendship. You have done plenty for me, *amica*. I return the favor. *Sì?*"

"I have no idea what I've done for you, but let's stick with the dress. Okay?" I hugged her. "Maybe I should wear black just to see the look on Mag's face when I walk down the aisle. Of course she'll be in mourning anyway. This wedding is her worst nightmare coming true."

"Jeremiah's parents? They will be here?" Flo studied me, trying to gauge my reaction to that.

"Jerry says they wouldn't miss it. I hope that doesn't mean Mag is planning to jump up when the minister asks if anyone has a reason why we shouldn't be wed." I laughed like I thought this was ridiculous. If only. Jer's mother had hated me on sight, and hundreds of years hadn't changed her first opinion. I was a lowly actress, not good enough for her high-born son.

"She wouldn't dare. Jeremiah would never forgive her. Am I right?" She linked her arm through mine. "I promise to stuff a bouquet in her mouth if she tries it. What do you think?"

"Sounds like a plan." I looked around. A few customers had taken an interest in our conversation. "It's early. Why don't we hit the mall and see if we can find something there that catches my eye."

"The mall? For a wedding dress?" Flo shuddered. "We need to fly to New York. Talk to a designer. Oh, I can't believe you left me with so little time."

"Jerry's impatient. He's waited a long, long, long time for me to say yes." I dragged her to the door and outside. "Humor me. We can at least look. I won't let you spend a fortune anyway. And help me brainstorm where we should have this wingding."

"Wing what?" Flo looked confused.

"Never mind." I hit the remote on my car that I'd left at the curb in front of the shop. "I mean the ceremony and reception. I want it to be special. Your wedding was perfect. But I can't do the same thing." I jumped in my car and got it started.

"Damian wouldn't mind. His hilltop makes a beautiful setting, no?" Flo slammed the passenger door.

"Of course. But I bet he's already planning the Winter Solstice Ball there. He never misses a year."

"Yes, my brother is very busy. I talked him into making the ball a masked costume party this year. I want to wear the necklace I got in Paris. You remember it?" Flo fussed with her seatbelt, making sure it didn't wrinkle her sweater. "I know I wore it on Halloween, but now it's my favorite piece. I must go as Marie again."

"Marie Antoinette? It was her necklace you had to sneak past customs when you flew from Paris?" Flo had gotten into some kind of hassle over the vintage piece. I could barely remember it. I'd had my own issues then. Jerry had had amnesia, and we'd been worried about how he'd react to his first plane ride when he was mentally stuck in the fifteenth century. He'd freaked out of course. Good times.

"That's the one. Don't you remember how beautiful it was?"

"Yes, sure. Gorgeous. I can't believe it really belonged to Marie Antoinette." Actually I'd been too wrapped up in keeping a burly Highlander from jumping out of a plane without a parachute at ten thousand feet to give it a good look. Then Halloween had been full of complications too. My life. Was it too much to hope that I could have a wonderful wedding go off without a hitch?

"Of course it did. I remember her wearing it. Sapphires the size of my thumbnail. *Squisito!*" Flo sighed. "Such a wonderful time. Too bad for Marie of course. I could have helped her escape. Turned her. But she was a silly chit. It amused her to have us around, of course. But to *become* a vampire? The thought revolted her. More than a guillotine? Pah!"

I shuddered. Flo had seen so much history. Of course so had I. I loved modern times and rarely looked back. "Costumes. See? Another thing to worry about. Have the invitations gone out yet?" I slammed on the brakes when a car zipped into the parking place I'd been aiming for. "Crap. I've got to do that too. Wedding invitations. But I have to nail down a place and time first. This is impossible."

"You can always elope." Flo looked behind us when a car honked. She let loose with some Italian and a hand gesture. "Kidding. Don't you dare. Like you say, you and Jeremiah have waited a long time, hundreds of years. So we celebrate. Big time. All of your friends will help you. Don't worry about it. Now promise you will listen to me in this mall. You are not fat. You are beautiful. No black. Too much like a funeral. No?"

"Okay. Just no white either." In the end the perfect dress was red. We found it in a high-end boutique, the only kind my pal would consider entering. Red was even a traditional color for a bride, if I'd been Chinese like the savvy salesgirl who'd waited on us. I didn't care what rationale we used. I felt good in the dress. It had the low neckline I loved and Flo approved. We bought it and some strappy sandals that worked with it. By the time we left the mall, the parking lot was emptying and we'd racked up a big bill. I didn't want to think how much. One thing crossed off my endless to-do list. We headed to N-V, the club my former bodyguard Rafe Valdez owned. Jerry and Richard were meeting us there.

We stopped by Flo's car and put our finds in her trunk. She was convinced I'd show the dress to Jerry otherwise, definitely unlucky before the wedding. Then I found a parking spot not too far down the block on Sixth Street and we headed for the door. We were about to go in when a man stepped out of the shadows. I recognized him immediately.

"Come. We have made our men wait long enough." Flo ignored the man who was suddenly at my elbow.

"Flo, have you met Miguel Cisneros?" I made the introductions, surprised when Flo didn't do her usual flirting when meeting a handsome man.

"I know him. Ricardo has told me who and what he is. Come, Glory. We go inside now." Flo ignored Miguel's smile and his outstretched hand. There was a short line but the doorman knew us both and had waved us in.

I saw by Miguel's suddenly serious face that I had better meet with him now, before I headed inside. He'd helped me once when I'd needed him and we had a deal. Guess it was time for me to hold up my end of the bargain. "I'll be in soon, Flo. Tell Jerry I'm in the bathroom fixing my hair or something." I grabbed her arm. "Don't mention Miguel."

"Keeping secrets from your fiancé already? Is it because you know you shouldn't be alone with him?" Flo had yet to speak to Miguel directly. "This is not a good idea." She actually tried to pull me to the door. "He is dangerous. Come inside."

I jerked my arm free. "My business with Miguel is *my* business. Now please leave me to it. If you want to tell Jer, go ahead. I'll deal with the fall-out." I gave her a warning look. Friends covered for friends and she knew it.

"Fine. I lie for you." She looked Miguel up and down. "You harm so much as a hair on Glory's head and I hunt you down like the dog you are and end you. *Entiendes*?"

"Tough talk, *chiquita*." Miguel wore a threatening face that made me put some space between us. I had forgotten for a minute just how dangerous he could be. "What have I ever done to you?"

"My husband has told me you are an assassin." Flo looked Miguel over. "I have had dealings with your kind before. My friend is good, clean. You are not fit to be in her company." Flo put her hand over mine. "Glory, you want me to stay?"

Miguel laughed at that. "Seriously? Are you going to protect Gloriana from big bad me?" He kept chuckling. "I'd like to see you try." He held his hands out to his sides. "Give it your best shot."

Flo rattled off something in Spanish that made Miguel's dark eyes harden. Then she glanced around at the crowd of mortals who had quit talking and were interested in our conversation.

"Would you two cool it? Flo, Miguel and I are, um," I searched for the right word, "friends. So go on inside and meet the guys. I'll be perfectly fine." I glanced meaningfully at the mortals who were openly gawking at us.

"You have been warned, *perro sucio*." She glared at Miguel then flounced inside, the tap of her high heels punctuating her threat.

"What did she call you?" I pulled Miguel over to the alley nearby to get away from our audience.

"A filthy dog. Is that fair? I swear I showered

before I came here tonight." Miguel grinned, obviously unfazed by the insult, and thrust his hands in his pockets. More than one girl in line sighed. He wore tight black jeans that hugged his taut butt and a matching cotton tee with a worn black leather jacket hanging open over it. Probably to blend into the night. He had the exotic looks of his Aztec ancestors and a body made for sin. I was immune for some reason, but most women weren't.

"Flo is my best friend and she was just being protective. I'll talk to her. Now, what do you want?"

"We had a deal, remember, Glory? I helped you when you had a little problem a while ago. Now it's time for some payback." He leaned against the brick wall, pretending to be casual, but I knew better. Despite the careless grin earlier, he was tense and I wondered what was up.

"Our deal." I so did not need this now. "You ready to do your part? You said you wanted to be accepted here in Austin. Join our straight society. That's going to be tough with your hard reputation, Miguel. Obviously people like Flo, the very people who have to accept you, think you're still working as a hit man." I shivered, and it wasn't from the chill. I wore a cute gray fleece jacket that I'd picked up on sale. Besides, vamps don't feel cold like humans do, and Austin's December night was mild. No, it was the idea that this man inches from me had killed dozens, maybe hundreds, of people for money that made me shudder.

"I've given it up. But you're right, my rep lingers and I still get calls. Got one just this week. That's really why I'm here." He glanced around and urged me deeper into the alley, away from prying eyes and interested mortals. "I'm doing you a favor. Though after that scene just now, I'm thinking taking the job might be doing the world a favor."

I was getting a really bad vibe from him. Not that he'd hurt me, but still… "Wait a minute. A hit? You got called for a hit? Miguel, you turned it down, didn't you?" I know, I'm supposed to be a bad ass vampire. But it was spooky in this dark, damp alley that smelled of garbage and rats. Miguel was standing close too. And I couldn't forget Flo's reaction. I had some skills, but he'd shown me before that his were just as good, maybe even better. I could try de-materializing and was about to do it when Miguel grabbed my arm. Smart. He'd anchored me, and I wasn't going anywhere. "How'd you know where to find me anyway?"

"This is one of your regular hangouts, isn't it? You're pretty predictable, Glory. Lucky for you the job wasn't about you. You'd be easy to hit." He smiled like he had all the answers.

"Then who the hell was it? I don't want to play games here, Miguel. Jerry's waiting for me." I admit I was getting more spooked by the second. A hit. Jerry's mother wouldn't hesitate to hire someone if she could be sure her son would never find out… She must be panicking now, thinking about me wedding the heir to Clan Campbell. She'd tried to take me out herself centuries ago. Flo was right though, she wouldn't risk alienating Jer now. But if she could arrange an "accident"…

"I can see what you're thinking. If anyone calls for a hit on you, I'll let you know. Just like I'm doing you the courtesy of dropping this information on you now. I told you, I'm out of the business." He leaned against the brick wall, pulled out a skinny cigar, and lit up. He took a deep draw, his dark eyes gleaming as he made me wait. "But I knew if I didn't accept this job, someone else would."

"Wait. You took the hit? Who are you going to kill, Miguel?" I grabbed his jacket. "Tell me before I beat it out of you." I probed his mind but he'd blocked it. Bastard. His shit-eating grin meant he was enjoying making me sweat.

"Your feisty little Italian buddy."

"Flo?" I fell back against the opposite wall. "What? Why?"

"She's a bitch but that's not why." He drew on his cigar and blew a smoke ring, watching it drift up toward the night sky. "Apparently she owns a piece of jewelry that someone sold her by mistake. There's a family that claims it's theirs. They contacted her. Demanded it back. Even agreed to reimburse her for her expenses. She's refused to give it up. Got pretty nasty about it. So they've decided to get it back the hard way."

"Wait. This is about a piece of jewelry?" I shook my head. "What piece?"

"Something she got in Paris last fall. It belonged to Marie Antoinette. That's the story going around anyway." He grinned around his cigar. "It's said to be cursed. Has been since the French queen got it from the family who is claiming it now. Here's a picture. Recognize it?" He held out his phone and there it was, the necklace Flo was so crazy about. The sapphires were huge. I was sure everyone who saw it on Halloween figured it had to be fake, a costume piece. No one at the party at N-V would have worn real jewels that valuable. It was obviously worth a fortune. No wonder she was so bent on wearing it now. If someone else wanted it, she was just stubborn enough to flaunt it.

"Oh, God. Yes, she has that necklace! She wore it on Halloween." I was shaking. Damn Flo. Of course she wouldn't just give back the necklace. She considered her jewels her insurance policy. She hoarded jewelry like it was gold bullion. When you live forever, she said, you had to put aside things that will last and hold their value. Jerry bought businesses and real estate. Richard owned stocks, antiquities and who knew what else. Me? I was lucky to have more than the clothes on my back. Living paycheck to paycheck did that to you.

"Yes, I remembered it as soon as I saw the photo. I've already confirmed that Florence has the bauble in her possession." He stubbed out the cigar with his heel. "She's pissed them off, Glory. At first they would have been satisfied with just the necklace. Or that's what they claim. Now they want her dead as well. Seems like the curse is true."

"So you agreed…" I realized the alley was swaying. No, that was me. I sat down on a wooden crate next to a Dumpster that reeked. "You can't kill her, Miguel."

"I don't want to. I know she's your friend. But if I hadn't taken the contract, another assassin would have picked up the job. It pays very well." He stood right in front of me, his jeans brushing against mine. "Look at me, Glory. If you want Flo to live, you're going to have to help me. Get her to give up the necklace. That's the first step."

"Oh, boy." I took his hand when he reached out to help me stand. "You know Richard actually paid for it. A small fortune I'm sure."

"Doesn't matter. The people who hired me have talked to Florence. The bill of sale is in her name. The man who sold it to her…" Miguel dropped my hand and paced the alley. "Well, he's been questioned."

"And?" I watched Miguel move silently. He was obviously thinking.

"These people are notorious. Let's just say they don't mess around. The man shouldn't have sold the piece. It was a pawn shop. He was supposed to hold it for the family. The arrangement is complicated but he broke their trust. He's been dealt with. But first he admitted that Florence's husband gave the necklace to her right in front of him. Made a big deal out of the gift."

"So if you don't kill her…" I wobbled on my high-heeled boots.

"They'll come after her themselves. They aren't paranormals, but they can hire them. The Maury family likes a slow kill. Pain and suffering make them feel like they've made their point. You know what I mean? So hiring a hit man was an act of kindness in their eyes." Miguel had his hands on my shoulders. "Are you all right?"

"No. We've got to fix this, Miguel." I looked up at him. "She's my best friend. Promise me you'll help me fix this."

"I came to you, didn't I?" He dropped a kiss on my forehead. "Now here's where you do your part. Get me an invitation to that Winter Solstice Ball. The one Florence's brother is hosting."

"Aw, hell. Seriously?" I backed up. "You see how she feels about you."

"But her brother is a businessman. Convince this

Damian Sabatini that I am one too. A man who can bring him more business. *Sí?*"

"But what kind of business? Loan sharking or Killers R Us?" I gasped when he gripped my shoulders.

"I'm into investments, real estate. Everything on the up and up from now on. So relax. I'm going straight. Any more hits come to me, I'll turn them down flat." Miguel's eyes bored into mine and I knew he was telling the truth. "You know you owe me. Hold up your end of the bargain and I'll see if I can save your friend Florence."

"Get your fucking hands off of Glory." Rafe was between us before I could gasp. He shoved Miguel until he hit the wall.

"Watch it, shifter. Glory, you want to call off your dog?" Miguel ignored Rafe's growl.

"Rafe, back off. Miguel and I were talking. No big deal." I put a soothing hand on Rafe's arm. He'd been my bodyguard for five years and more than that for a short time. He was still one of my best friends. I guess his doorman had told him I'd disappeared into the alley instead of coming inside. I knew he didn't like or trust Miguel. No one in the Austin paranormal community did. Which was going to make my part of our deal hard to work out.

"I saw him pin you. You look upset." Rafe vibrated with the need to put his fist in Miguel's grinning face. It didn't take a mind reader to see that.

"He gave me some bad news. He's actually doing me a favor. So calm down. Please." I rubbed his arm, trying to soothe him. "You need to get over this kneejerk reaction to Miguel. He and I are working together on a little project. He assures me he's going legit. Aren't you, Miguel?" I blasted both of them with a smile that dared them to start swinging. "I want my friends to get along."

"Legit? Doing what? And I can't imagine Blade will allow you to have anything to do with Cisneros once you're married."

Miguel laughed. "Allow? Oh, you did not just say that." He eased down the alley, hands up. "Glory, talk to you later. I'm holding off. Talk to your friend. The female one. You have my number. Call me. But the clock is ticking. We need this situation resolved by Christmas."

"You're kidding." I glanced at my watch. Stupid. Because I didn't need a watch to tell me that we had just a few weeks to figure out Flo's situation. I decided to deal with one problem at a time.

"I can't believe you're consorting with that piece of shit." Rafe tried to pull me toward the side entrance to the club a few feet down the alley.

"Hold it." I dug in my heels. "Miguel is right about one thing. What do you mean 'allow'? Jerry doesn't allow or not allow me to consort with anyone. I am and will remain my own woman. Got it?" I poked him in the chest.

"Explain what kind of business you could possibly have with a loan shark and hit man then." Rafe let go of me. "Have you lost your mind? You need money, you come to me or to your fiancé."

"It's not a money thing. He's not a loan shark anymore and he's been trying to stop taking hits." I tossed my hair back over my shoulders to avoid Rafe's sharp gaze. Yes, he was still a good friend but he was always trying to protect me, whether I wanted him to or not. Once a bodyguard, always a bodyguard, I guess.

He slapped his thigh. "Now that's rich. *Trying* to stop? What the hell does that mean? He just takes a few hits for old time's sake?" His laugh was bitter. "Get a clue, Glory. He's a stone cold killer. Hang with a guy like that and you might as well paint a target on your pretty chest." He reached out and drew one on my right breast.

"Stop it!" I slapped his hand. "Leave me alone. I'm perfectly safe with Miguel. Everyone knows he's a dangerous man, including me. I watch my back around him. Did you forget I have some awesome powers? I can turn *him* to stone if he threatens me." I crossed my fingers behind my back, leaving out the fact that Miguel was the only paranormal I knew who could do the same thing and break that freeze if he needed to. Maybe I *did* need the kind of reality check my pal Rafe could always provide. I resisted the urge to pour out my troubles e. No, we'd both moved on and he didn't need my problems on his shoulders.

"Then do that. But much as I hate the phrase, remember that if you lie down with dogs, you'll get up with fleas." Rafe looked me up and down, like he was checking me for bugs already.

"Oh, please. Think about it. He can certainly make sure I'm safe from any other threat when I'm with him. Since you're no longer my bodyguard, it's kind of nice to have someone else watch my back." I added a hair toss for emphasis. Didn't phase him.

"I thought that's what Blade did now. You *are* marrying him. Is that still on?" He grabbed my left hand and stared at my ring. "Guess so."

"Yes. New Year's Day. I hope you'll come. Bring a date." I stared at the ring too. It was real. I pasted on a happy smile.

"Sure, count me in. Invite Caine. You can have a chorus of your discarded lovers there to sing at your wedding." He jerked open the door into the club. "Get in here. Since your new boy is gone, you'd better not hang out in this deserted alley. You have a habit of getting into trouble in alleys."

I rolled my eyes but stalked into the club ahead of him. Men! I saw his current girlfriend waiting for him at the bar. She looked at us, her eyes a little too bright. Oh, no. I wasn't going to have her getting any wrong ideas. I smiled and headed her way.

"Lacy, I don't know how you stand this man. I just got a lecture on the company I keep." I glanced up toward the balcony. Yes, my man and Flo's had settled in with drinks at their usual table. Rafe kept blood with alcohol stocked for his vampire customers.

"When he tries to boss me around, I just ignore him." She smiled and linked her arm through mine. A were-cat, she worked as my day manager and had been dating Rafe for a while now. "Rafe, you might as well give it up. Modern women do not obey."

"I so get that." He gestured and the bartender set a glass in front of him. "It was a lot easier back in the day."

"Oh, yes, we never forget that you're ancient." Lacy made a face. "So's Glory, but she's rolled with the times." She squeezed my arm. "Guess you decided Mr. Blade has too or you wouldn't be marrying him."

"He's still a work in progress, but I think he's come along well." I saw him wave and give me a look that meant come on up. Flo was laughing at something Richard was whispering in her ear. My stomach twisted. How was I going to get her to give up her necklace? And would just returning it satisfy that bloodthirsty family now?

"They've set a date, New Year's Day. You'll come with me to the wedding, won't you, babe?" Rafe pulled Lacy to him, sliding his arm around her waist.

"Sure." She looked up at him, clearly more than a little in love.

One of Lacy's sisters was standing right down the bar from her, watching us. Lace had several sisters, brothers too. I wondered what they thought of her relationship with a shifter who wasn't a member of the cat family.

"Of course Lacy and all of my shop crew will be invited." I smiled and gestured toward the balcony. "Now I need to go on up."

"Wait a minute. Seems like we hardly ever see each other. Me working days, you nights." Lacy sipped a glass of what looked like water. "Do you remember my sister DiDi?" she said when her sister moved closer.

"Sure. Nice to see you." When a waiter waved at Rafe. he murmured an excuse and left. "There goes your date. It's not easy dating the club owner, is it, Lace?"

"No." Her shoulders slumped. "Our dates are never uninterrupted when we're here. It's a good thing…" She glanced at her sister. "Well, guess I might as well let the cat out of the bag, so to speak."

"What?" DiDi glanced at me. "She called me over here with news. You still have a job, don't you, Sis?"

"Sure. But I lost my apartment. Mr. Blade evicted me. He's making a giant place for Glory and him on the second floor of our building. So I had to make other arrangements." Lacy smiled suddenly. "Rafe and I are living together now. Isn't that great?"

DiDi hissed and I swear her hair rose a good three inches. I backed up a step. "Are you nuts? Mom will kill you." DiDi signaled the bartender. "Tequila, a double."

"I think that's great." I kissed Lacy's cheek. "Congratulations. That's a big step." There had been a time when *I'd* been Rafe's number one. But now he'd obviously found a way to move on. I was happy for him.

"Di's right. Mom is going to stroke out. Shifters and were-cats? That's a non-starter for Mom-cat." Lacy leaned against the bar. "She's been planning my wedding for years, but I won't accept any of the mates she's picked out for me. Boring tabbies or randy alley cats. No thank you. But Rafe..." She sighed, her eyes dreamy. "I know you won't kiss and tell, Glory, but you should understand. Rafe is so much more than just a shifter. He's, um, special."

DiDi downed one of her shots, then signaled for another. "Girl, you are unleashing a shitstorm. Warn me when you go to tell Mom. I want to be out of town."

I just stared at Lacy. Remembering. Yes, Rafe was special. But I'd let him go and made my choice-- the man who waited for me upstairs. I patted Lacy's shoulder. Said something encouraging and headed up. I couldn't keep every guy I'd ever wanted on a string forever. They had to move on because I sure had.

Flo smiled when I slipped into a chair next to

Jerry. "Let me see your ring again, *mi amica*. I have been telling Jeremiah. A woman should have good jewelry. If he hasn't bought you a Christmas present yet, he should add to your collection. It is your security, no?"

"Gloriana doesn't have to worry about that now, Florence. She's finally agreed to let me take care of her." Jerry dropped a kiss on my lips. "Don't hurt me now. You know what I mean, sweetheart."

"Yes. I get it, Jer. We'll be equal partners in this marriage. And you don't have to buy me a boatload of jewelry to prove your love." I snuggled against him.

"Hush, Glory. A wise woman never turns down good jewelry. Who knows what the future might hold? As I say, security. We must take care of ourselves." Flo held my fingers and studied my diamond. "Ricardo understands this and is happy to make me feel loved with his generosity." She dropped my hand and kissed Richard to prove her point. He didn't seem to mind her frank talk.

Security. I wasn't familiar with the concept. Jerry's arm tightened around my shoulders. He knew how I felt. I'd struggled against being dependent on anyone, even him, but some part of me craved never having to worry about my next meal, a roof over my head, safety. Jerry offered me that feeling. Flo had Richard and yet she still hoarded jewels "just in case."

I swallowed some of the synthetic blood with alcohol in the drink Jerry had ordered for me. It did little to chase away the cold in the pit of my stomach. Flo was never going to give that necklace away willingly. Still, I was going to try honesty first. Ask her to give it up. If that didn't work? Well, then I'd have to deceive my best friend. Not easy around a mind-reading vampire.

THREE

"What was going on down there?" Jerry kept his arm around me. "Lots of hugging and drinking going on."

"Lacy moved in with Rafe. They're officially a couple now. I was happy about that. Her sister? Not so much." I picked up the glass of blood with alcohol again. "Mmm. Thanks, I needed that."

"You sure it didn't bother *you* that Valdez has moved on?" Jerry watched me closely. Jealousy?

"No, not that. Driving over here was a little nerve-wracking. Right, Flo?" I looked to her for help.

"Yes! Everywhere we go there are crazy drivers. I wonder if Glory should be driving one of those big SUBs. Her little car would be squashed like a bug if a truck hits her." Flo smacked her hand on the table for emphasis.

"I think you mean SUV, darling." Richard

rescued her drink when it almost spilled. "And I know what you mean. The freeways are chaos. I hate the idea of either of you in a small car out there."

"Do you want a bigger car, Gloriana? I'll buy you one." Jerry slid his hand down my arm, keeping me from picking up my glass again. I realized I'd already almost drained it. "You seem a little rattled. What happened?"

"Oh, it was nothing. Just an eighteen wheeler getting a little close, that's all." I patted his hand. As an excuse, I thought it worked. I was blocking my thoughts. No reason for him to see I was really upset about Flo. "Don't you dare buy me a car. I don't want to drive one of those enormous things. I can't even climb into one without showing the world my underwear when I'm in a short skirt."

Jerry grinned. "I don't mind seeing your underwear. But not sure I want 'the world' to have the privilege."

Flo was eyeing me. She knew I was covering up something—the meeting with Miguel for sure. "Well, I don't want one either. Both of us look very good in our little convertibles when we put the top down. Now I got Glory here to you. Tell us about your surprise. What have you two been up to?"

"We scouted some wedding venues. And I think we found the perfect one." Richard pulled a thin laptop from a leather messenger bag I hadn't noticed hanging from the back of his chair. "Take a look." He quickly brought up a page. I had to admire his computer speed. My laptop was old, overloaded and took forever just to boot up.

"Oh, Glory, look. It's like a Tuscan villa perched on a hilltop." Flo turned the screen toward me. "It would be most romantic at night, with the lights of Austin twinkling in the distance."

"Wow. What is this place?" I stared at the picture. It *was* a villa, a perfect replica of one that you might see in Italy. Of course their website showed it sparkling in the sun but there were a variety of pictures of weddings by candlelight on the terrace and one next to a waterfall. "Jerry! What do you think?"

"I think I'd marry you next to a cactus in Death Valley. But this place was actually great. Richard and I shifted out there. It has an old world feel I liked, even though someone built it fairly recently. I think we can get it New Years' Day. I'll book it if you think it'll do." He scooted his chair next to mine. "Is this really happening? Are you actually going to commit to me this time?"

"Yes. And this place is perfect." I tore my gaze from a slide show of weddings with glowing brides and happy grooms taking vows beneath a canopy of stars. Grabbing Jerry's hands I looked into his eyes and showed him my thoughts. I wanted this, wanted him. And I didn't doubt it was time to make this happen.

"I'll call them and confirm." Richard had his arm around Flo. "As best man it's the least I can do. Look at them, Florence. They're actually acting like a happy couple."

"Yes. I am thrilled." Flo touched a cocktail napkin to her eyes. "I'm going to throw you a shower that will drown you in presents, *mia amica*. What kind you want? Lingerie? Or more practical things? I lived with you, remember? Your towels? Rags, I say."

"We're running out of time, you know. But that's a sweet thought." I let go of Jerry's hand. Richard had stepped away from the table and was on the phone. I was surprised the venue was open this late but I guess if they were hosting a wedding tonight, they would be.

"I'll manage. Make a guest list and leave the rest to me." Flo typed something on the computer, and I had to admit I was surprised she even used one. "I'm going on-line now. You must register everywhere. Have you done it?"

"Uh, no." I glanced around to make sure no mortals could hear us. "I mean what does a vampire need? Dishes? Certainly not pots and pans. It seems silly--"

"*Silencio!* Nothing about marrying your soulmate is silly. Am I right, Jeremiah?" She gave Jerry a look that dared him to disagree.

"No, of course not. This is going to be the most important night of my life." He kissed my lips.

"Jerry!" I had to admit I'd been hanging back, letting him see to details I should have been more involved with. "It's important to me too. Thank you. I'm sure it will be perfect." I touched his cheek, savoring the texture of his evening beard.

"It will be if I have anything to do with it." Jerry's smile worried me. I knew that look. He was up to something. "I have another surprise for you, Gloriana. Look." Jerry got to his feet. "Here he comes now."

When I saw who was sauntering up the stairs, I poked Jerry in the arm. "You didn't!"

"Oh, yes, I did. Meet your wedding singer." Jerry rubbed his bicep though I knew he considered my feeble hit a love tap. "Ow. I think you bruised me."

"Good." I met the man at the top of the stairs. "Ray! Why...?"

Israel Caine, nickname Ray, pulled me into a hug that turned Jerry's grin into a frown. "Why am I here? How could I miss your wedding? I have to be there in case you come to your senses and decide to bolt. I'll help you get away. We can shift to Tahiti and lie naked on a beach together." Ray ignored my efforts to put some space between us. "When your fiancé asked me to sing..?" Ray finally let me go with a pat on the butt. "Hey, nothing I like better than singing to you, babe."

"Maybe this wasn't such a good idea." Jerry jerked me to his side.

"Oh, no. I love it. It will make the night just perfect." I sent my man a mental message to let me go. Jerry put out his hands, giving me some space. "You started this and you should have remembered that Israel Caine doesn't do anything without attitude."

"You so get me, sweet thing." Ray grinned and pulled out a chair. His "don't give a shit" attitude this time didn't fool me one bit. He was a little steamed, but he wasn't about to let Jerry see it.

"You don't have to do this, Ray. I know you're a busy man." I knew he wasn't nursing a broken heart and neither was I. We were friends and had settled that a while back.

"Never too busy for you, Glory girl. If you are determined to marry this throwback to the dark ages, then I'll sing whenever and whatever you want." He winked at me, letting me know he was enjoying pulling Jerry's chain.

"Good to know." I moved over to stand behind Jerry when he sat down again, my hands firmly on his shoulders. I could feel the tension in them. He was right to be jealous of Ray. What on earth had possessed him to drag the singer into this?

"I say we make it a duet." Ray sat down and motioned to a waitress. She knew what he liked. Every waitress at N-V was half in love with him and had been since he'd performed there the first time. He and Rafe weren't best buds, but since Ray had made Austin one of his homes, he liked to try out new songs at this club that catered to vampires. Rafe wasn't about to turn down good business, and a famous rock star brought in the bucks.

I was Ray's mentor. It had taken him a long time to come to terms with the vampire life since he'd been turned against his will. Now he was mentoring his own fledgling vampire. Payback was a bitch as they say.

"A duet? Maybe. Is Sienna still in town? A duet with her would be better. As the bride I'll be pretty busy." I settled into my chair again since Jerry had calmly picked up his drink and hadn't made a move for one of his knives. Sienna Star was the new vampire Ray was now responsible for. I'd turned her, but Ray had accidentally drained her. That had left him stuck with her as far as I was concerned. I hated making new vampires and Sienna hadn't exactly embraced her new role, not without causing problems.

"Yes, she's here. And giving me fits. She'd still like nothing better than to out all vampires. If the label hadn't threatened to pull her next album, I'm afraid she'd already have had a press conference about it." Ray leaned back in his chair. "You're right. I should bring her to the wedding. Work up a duet with her."

He smiled as the waitress set his glass in front of him. No alcohol for him, he was a recovering alcoholic. At least I hoped he was still on the wagon. I casually picked up his glass and sniffed.

"Hey, you don't have to do that. I'm still clean. Sienna's giving me enough shit that I need a clear head."

I relaxed and handed him back the drink, synthetic blood and the highest quality. "Sorry. You know I worry about you."

"Can we get on with our plans?" Jerry practically growled. "Gloriana certainly doesn't need to sing at her own wedding. Caine, you and Sienna Star doing a duet. Perfect. Right, darling?" He slung his arm around me in a death grip.

"Yes. I'll have enough to worry about that night. I have to look as good as possible and then there are those out-of-town guests to entertain." I grimaced. "Flo, what are you doing?"

"Registering you. Give me a color for the bathrooms. And bedroom linens. This is such fun." Her eyes were shining. "Ricardo, I think I divorce you and we do it again. Marry. I didn't register last time. I want to do this."

"No, darling. You're stuck with me." Richard was grinning as he put away his phone. "We have New Year's Day at eleven pm. Now you can order invitations. I'll email you the details, Gloriana."

"Stick with neutrals, Flo. Sheets too. No satin." I glanced at Ray, some memories surfacing. "Too slippery."

"Neutrals are boring. Ricardo, you love my pink sheets, don't you?" Flo teased her husband as she filled in a bridal registration for me. I just sat back and listened. Ray was goading Jerry, suggesting songs that he knew my Scot would hate sung at his wedding. One was "Glory Girl", a song Ray had written just for me. If Ray even hinted that he and I had been together once... I'd never told Jerry about that. My nerves suddenly got the best of me.

"Stop it! I don't even know the difference between a fingertip towel and a hand towel. And who cares whether it's ecru or beige? You're right, Flo, they're both boring but I can't make a decision right now. Ray, sing something romantic. You should know what I like. And quit trying to make Jerry pull out one of his knives." I jumped up. "Come on, Flo. Ladies room. Now." Marriage. I'd run from it for four hundred years. Why? I don't know. Fear of monogamy forever? I wasn't a slut but the idea suddenly sounded overwhelming. The four of them stared at me when I grabbed Flo's arm.

"But I'm only halfway done, *amica.*"

"Looks like a case of nerves to me. Second thoughts, Glory?" Ray chuckled. Oh, hell, he'd put this on Jerry and there'd be a fight. I didn't care. I needed to talk to Flo.

"Flo has lipstick on her teeth. And we need to talk about colors before she commits on this registry. It's an important decision. Right, Flo?"

She didn't hear me. She was scrubbing her front teeth with her index finger.

"How long? Oh, I hate to see anyone with lipstick on a tooth. It is so ugly." Flo kept muttering as she let me drag her with me.

At the bottom of the stairs, I finally let go. "Not the ladies room. Rafe's office. I can see he's at the bar with Lacy. Come on." Flo just followed me through the crowd on the dance floor to where I knew Rafe kept a soundproof office. I could feel her studying me. The lipstick story had obviously not held up when she'd seen her finger come away clean.

"Is not nerves, is it, Glory?" she said as soon as I closed us both inside. "You love Jeremiah. I know you are ready to marry him."

"Yes, I am. But I want you there, by my side." I grabbed her shoulders and shoved her into a chair. I was telling the truth. I was actually ready for monogamy. But this Flo thing? I couldn't just sit around drinking and picking out linens when I had a life and death issue unresolved.

"Hey, what are you doing?" Flo dragged my hand off of her. "You almost ripped my dress."

"Sorry." I paced the floor in front of her. Straight talk. That was the only way to deal with this. "Did someone contact you about your necklace? The one that belonged to Marie Antoinette?"

"What? How do you know..?" She looked up from examining her sleeve. Okay so I'd gotten a little rough. But I hadn't ripped anything. "Did that Cisneros say something?" She jumped up, bumping into me because I was standing too close. "He's a hit man. Have they put out a contract on me? *Madre de Dios*!" She crossed herself and began speaking rapid Italian.

"Slow down. Speak English. Obviously you know what I'm talking about." I sank into one of the two leather chairs across from Rafe's messy desk.

"Of course I do. These people. They call me. Don't ask how they get my number. It is unlisted." She threw up her hands, muttering more Italian. "*Non é importante.* Anyway, they call me. Start making demands. Like I have to give up my beautiful necklace that Ricardo paid good money for." She sank into the chair next to me. "I tell you. Why should I listen to them?"

"Because now they want to kill you, Flo." I grabbed her hand. "Miguel is trying to go straight. Give up the killing game. But they didn't know that. Apparently they just knew he was the go-to guy in this area of the country and he has a," I swallowed, sick at the thought of what this meant, "good reputation for getting the job done. Anyway, they contacted him when you wouldn't play ball. They put out the contract. As a favor to me, he said he'd look into it."

"You mean he took their money." Flo gripped my hand until I had to pry away her fingers. She was hurting me. Couldn't blame her.

"He's trying to help me save your life, buddy. Listen to me. The first thing we have to do is return that damned necklace."

"No." Her mouth was set in a firm line. "They have no claim. I knew Marie. She got the necklace as a gift from an admirer. The Maurys must have sold it to him. Now they want it back? Too bad for them."

"No, Flo. Too bad for you. I'd say the admirer must have stolen it. The man who sold it to you wasn't supposed to let it go. He's been, uh, punished."

"Saul? What have they done to him? I have been buying jewels from him for years." For the first time Flo actually looked upset. "He is a kind man. I forced him to sell to me. Once I saw the piece... Well, I remembered it. Had to have it. Marie and I were friends. Yes, she was silly, but had a kind heart. What they did to her... It has haunted me." She looked around and grabbed a paper towel from a stack next to the door to dab at her eyes. "So long ago. You'd think I'd get used to losing my mortal friends."

"Focus, Flo. I don't like losing friends either. But be sensible. Give the necklace back. It's only a thing. It certainly doesn't bring your friend back. And it might not satisfy these people either since you've really pissed them off."

Flo tossed down the wadded up towel. "Well, they've pissed me off too." She took a steadying breath, her eyes blazing as she jumped to her feet. "Are they vampire? I'd like to see them come after me themselves. Hiding behind hit men. Pah! We will see how brave they are. I call Saul. See if he is okay. I take revenge if he is not."

"Are you going to tell Richard about this?" I knew I would if she didn't. Surely he'd talk some sense into her.

Flo narrowed her gaze on me. "Why do you ask? The necklace is mine. You make a big deal about independence. Am I right? Should I run to Ricardo with my little problem?"

"It's not a *little* problem. And Richard could help us solve it. Get real, Flo. We have to appease these ruthless people. What's all this talk about revenge? For a pawn shop owner in Paris? You have to save your own butt first, girlfriend. Don't you get that?"

"Us? It is not us in trouble, Glory. It is me. Stay out of it. I will take care of the matter." She stomped to the door and kicked it. The fact that she was probably damaging her high-heeled boots was evidence that she was truly upset. "I appreciate the warning. I do. But I am not returning the necklace.

Tell your friend Miguel, the hitman, to deliver that message to those people. And, if you are truly my friend, you will not breathe a word of this to Ricardo. Are we agreed?"

"I can't--" The look in her eyes stopped me cold. My happy Italian had a dark side and I didn't want to mess with her.

"As for that pawn shop owner. I know him a long time, *tu mi capisci*? He has earned my trust and my loyalty. If you were in trouble, I do the same. Help you or get revenge if I am too late." Flo suddenly reached out and pulled me to her chest. "You came to me. I love you for it. Now stay away. Let me handle it. I will not die. No worry," She pulled back, pasted on a fake smile and took a shuddery breath.

"I can't just turn that worry off, Flo. This is a big deal." I blinked back tears I couldn't allow myself to shed.

"I know. I will figure it out. Now you must show that you are still a good actress. We cannot let the men know we have a problem." She muttered something in Italian, pulled a lipstick out her purse and expertly drew it across her lips. "There. Now we must go back." She jerked open the door. "Come, smile. You are a good friend but you cannot tell me what to do."

I shook my head then staggered back to the chair. I wasn't ready to follow her yet, a smile was beyond me. There had to be another way to deal with this. I just wished I knew what it was. I pulled my phone out of my pocket. Yes, I did have his number. And what did that say about me? A hit man on speed dial. Shit.

FOUR

"**What's** going on with you and Florence?" Jerry and I were lying in his big king-sized bed. He'd made love to me until I was boneless. Now I needed to get dressed and go to the shop. We were living at his house until the apartment was ready. I had two things on my list tonight that I had to accomplish--order wedding invitations and pick out a costume for the Winter Solstice Ball. For some reason both those decisions overwhelmed me, so I'd stalled getting out of bed and enjoyed some alone time with Jerry instead.

"I don't know what you mean." I decided I'd better get in the shower. I couldn't discuss Flo's situation with Jerry. He'd tell Richard and then the rift between Flo and me would be even wider.

"Come on, you two were together every night planning for the wedding until we met the other night at N-V. Then you dragged her downstairs and she hasn't called or come around since." Jerry rolled over and watched me gather up the clothes he'd dropped on the way to bed and start hanging them up.

"We had a little disagreement. She's bossy. You saw her registering me, us, like she was the bride." I couldn't look at Jerry while I made up this excuse. "It's my wedding. Right? She was trying to take over. I finally told her to back off. Give me some space." I stepped into the walk-in closet so he couldn't see that I was near tears. I hated lying to him but the truth wasn't an option. I threw his shirt into a hamper and found a hanger for his jeans. My clothes took up a small section of the huge walk-in. It was a symbol of how our lives were so unequal. Jerry had so much and I'd bring so little to our marriage. The tears that were so near the surface lately threatened to fall. Pity party. I was so ready to toot the horn and toss the confetti.

"I thought you two were having fun together." Jerry stood right behind me, his hands sliding around my waist. "You sure you're not just nervous about the wedding? Is it bothering you that my folks are coming?"

"Of course it is." I whirled around and buried my face in his warm strong chest. God, but I loved the smell and feel of him. His strength. Just having him hold me made everything feel more...manageable. "Your mother hates me. She's going to try to ruin this wedding if she can."

"Gloriana, settle down." Jerry smoothed my back, his touch calming me as it always did. "Mum will not do a damned thing to ruin our night. I'll see to it. I've talked to her and let her know how important this is to me. She will put on a happy smile and be gracious or, by God, I'll never speak to her again." He lifted my chin so I could see his eyes and read his mind. "Do you believe me?"

"Yes." I kissed him then, deeply, tasting him and savoring the delicious connection we had. "Thank you, Jer. I know how much family means to you."

"*You* are my family, Gloriana. Now and forevermore. You can take that as my vow. Whether it is in front of a preacher and our friends or not." He was deadly serious and I loved him more than I ever had.

"Jerry." I pulled him down to the floor, desperate to have him again. Would I ever tire of the feel of his hard body against mine? I couldn't imagine it.

He touched me in all the places he knew drove me wild. I kissed a path down his strong chest to the burgeoning proof that he wanted me as much as I did him. I pushed him back and took him into my mouth, drawing him deep inside as I squeezed his sacs and breathed in his essence. He was mine, eager to prove that he would have no other. It gave me a power that made me stroke him faster, with a rougher touch. Then I bit deep into the vein at his upper thigh. His blood was warm, salty and like heaven to me. His shout of pleasure made my own satisfaction double, triple, until I quivered with it. I needed... more. So I turned until he could use his clever mouth on me. Oh, God, but he knew me. He held me in place, his tongue just where he could bring me to crest after crest.

I pulled back, sitting astride him, groaning as his cock plunged deep inside me. Yes! This is what I wanted, needed, loved. My man, my lover, my husband. I couldn't wait to take my own vow. Yes, he'd be mine forevermore too.

#

By the time I got to the shop it was almost midnight. At least the Internet never closed and after dithering over font, paper, and style, I finally managed to order the invitations on-line. Then I took advantage of owning my own resale shop. We specialized in carrying a variety of costumes so I had plenty to choose from. One of them should be perfect to wear to Damian Sabatini's annual Winter Solstice Ball. But there was one problem. I really, really wanted my best friend's help making a choice. I punched speed dial for Flo and was relieved when she answered.

"Are you going to lecture me?" Her voice had a chill I hated.

"No. I've missed you. Any chance you can come by the shop and give me some advice on what to wear to Damian's party?" I had pulled a few options but none of them were singing to me. Of course this had just been an excuse to call my best friend. We needed to mend this rift between us. And I was dying to know what was going on with the threat against her.

"I've missed you too. I hope you've worked on the guest list for your shower. I'm still planning it, you know." Flo's voice sounded shaky. She'd obviously thawed. "I am coming now. Stay there. It will be a few minutes." She ended the call.

"Florence is coming here?" Miguel stood a few feet away. He was examining the rack of men's evening wear.

"When did you sneak in here?" I stuck my phone in my jeans pocket. "You going to talk to Flo about her, um, problem?" I glanced around. Midnight was a dead time in my business, though we'd been busy earlier when the shifts had changed at nearby hospitals.

"You bet I am. She called the pawn shop owner." He must have seen my surprise. "Yes, he's still alive, but barely. Apparently he has lots of valuable contacts in our world so the Maurys are afraid to alienate them by killing him outright." Miguel smiled at my furtive peeks around us. "Yes, I checked too. Your clerk is taking a smoke break in the alley and we are very much alone."

"Good thing. Both that we aren't being overheard and that Saul is alive. Flo was ready to rip open some throats over her buddy Saul. Apparently he generates a lot of loyalty." I carried my costume choices to the back room. Sure enough, I could smell shape-shifter Megan's bad habit through the back door.

"Yes, the Maurys are now very much aware. Flo called them too. The woman is ballsy, I'll give her that. She's declared war on them. Refuses to give up her necklace and dares them to try to hit her. You can imagine how that went over."

"So what now?" I sighed. This could not end well.

"I'm waiting for my invitation then I'll tell you. Have you talked to Sabatini yet?" Miguel stalked out to the shop. "I heard it's a costume party. I like this jacket. Maybe I'll do a Rhett Butler look with a top hat. You have one of those?" He slipped on a vintage wine-colored velvet jacket that fit him perfectly. The color wasn't bad with his dark skin either. "I don't keep much stuff from my past. I move around a lot."

"You're kidding me. You're going to wear a

costume? Mix and mingle with Flo's brother while you are committed to a hit on her?" I stalked over to a locked case, pulled the key from my other pocket, the one without my phone, and opened it. The vintage silk hat was expensive but I knew Miguel could afford it and I could use the cash flow. "See if this fits your enormous head."

He just grinned and pushed it on over his dark hair. "Perfect. Now a white silk shirt and a cravat. I have tux pants. That'll do it, I think."

"You are quite a piece of work." I pulled out the perfect shirt in his size—I'd become an expert in figuring that out—and a man's navy silk scarf. "Tie this scarf into a cravat style. It'll give you the look you're after. And I have a stickpin that'll finish it off." I unlocked another case and pulled out a pearl pin that would add to his total cost in a major way. He didn't blink at the price tag, just handed it to me.

"Fix it for me. You know I can't use a mirror."

"Yeah, right." I adjusted the scarf, stuck in the pin and stepped back. Yep, a dark and dangerous Rhett Butler. If my next door neighbor Diana came as Scarlett like she usually did, they'd make quite a pair. Maybe Damian, who dated Diana and tended to take her for granted, needed some competition. "That's the look. Ladies will swoon. *If* I can get you in."

"Call Damian now. I want to hear you do it." He sat in front of the register on a stool we kept for customers.

"Fine. All I can promise is that I'll try. He may not be eager to associate with a known criminal." I pulled out my phone. Of course I had Damian's number in my contact list. He was a supplier for the best synthetic blood. I couldn't afford it, but Jerry and

Ray and all the well-heeled vamps used him. I had to admit, being married to Jerry would mean I'd be drinking the premium stuff from now on as well. Jer wouldn't have my bargain brand in his fridge.

Damian and I had had a moment when I'd first arrived in Austin. He was known as Casanova, a myth he worked hard to live up to. He was handsome, Italian, and had a line that made most women weak in the knees. I hadn't been immune. Now, I was all about Jerry. Damian and I had established a nice friendship, mostly because of his sister Florence. He answered on the second ring.

"Gloriana, Jeremiah already called me. He said both of you are coming to my ball. Is he going to trot out his plaid again?" Damian chuckled. Everyone knew Jerry didn't care for costumes and used his clan plaid as his dress of choice whenever a costume was called for.

"You know Jerry. I'm still working on my look. No plaid for me. Makes my butt look big."

"Ridiculous. Your butt is *perfetto*." Damian had always been appreciative of a full figure. He and Diana had been an item for a long time and she had some extra inches almost everywhere.

"Thank you. Glad you think so. Now as to why I called. I have a friend who would like to get to know you better. He thought an invitation to your ball might be the way to do that." I glanced at Miguel who was obviously listening to both sides of the conversation. Ears like a bat. He had taken off his purchases and now laid them on the counter.

"And who is this friend? Does Jeremiah know him?"

"Yes. Sort of. It's Miguel Cisneros."

"The hit man?" If I didn't know better, I'd say Damian had dropped his phone. "You call him your *friend?*"

"He's not a hit man any more, Damian. You know people can change. You've changed yourself. Look how you've settled down. Head of the local vampire council now. Not the wild party boy you used to be, are you?" I grinned when I heard a spate of Italian.

"Don't remind me. I think I am losing my touch. I should move back to Italia, race sports cars again, go back to my fast women. I am turning into a staid boring pillar of the community." He spat this like he was disgusted.

"No, it's a good thing. You will live longer, not being chased by irate husbands. Right?"

"Hah! I am a dead shot, a fencing master. And don't even ask me how mortal men fare when they try to come after me." Big sigh. "So why does Cisneros want to meet me and what's in it for me?"

Miguel grabbed my phone. "Sabatini, Cisneros here. Gloriana was kind enough to provide the introduction. Let me plead my own case."

"I'm listening." Damian didn't say anything else.

"I understand you're a businessman. So am I. Not what I used to do, of course. That is finished. No more loansharking either. I cut all ties with Lucky Carver and her kind. But the years I worked for her, I learned some valuable lessons and made some contacts that could be useful for both of us."

"How?" Damian was being unusually curt.

"Many people I know are vampires, of course. Good clients for your synthetic blood operation. Also, I have a considerable amount of capital I would like to invest. I understand you are into real estate in Austin and elsewhere in the state. I think we could work together to pick up some property, turn a profit. But we'd need to sit down in the same room to discuss that." Miguel said something in what I assumed was Italian.

Damian answered in the same language and I was out of it then. I barely speak English. Foreign languages have always defeated me. I began writing down the list of Miguel's purchases on a bill of sale. By the time I got to the total, Miguel had ended the call.

"So, are you going to the ball?"

"Yes. And we are going to meet sooner than that to discuss some business. Seems we have more in common than Sabatini thought. A love of fast cars and fast women, among other things." Miguel was grinning. "I'm thinking we should start a fencing club. I've missed a good match with a sword." He glanced at my total and peeled off some bills.

"Good grief, you and Damian really are two peas in a pod." Cash sale. I took the money and slipped it into the register.

"We both understand how to make a buck. Thanks, Glory, for keeping your end of our deal." Miguel took the bag with his purchases.

"I can't believe you're going into business with my brother." Flo stood inside the front door. "I doubt he'll follow through with these plans if you kill me."

Megan walked in from the back room. "I'm back from break, Glory."

"Great. Let's take this to the back room, people." I dragged Flo toward my storeroom. Miguel sauntered after us after giving Megan an interested once-over. She smiled at him. She was attractive and single.

"Quit dragging me, Glory. I'm going." Flo peeled my fingers off of her arm and stepped into the room.

"This is going to be fun." Miguel gestured for me to go ahead of him. "Megan, is it? What time do you get off work?" He winked.

"Leave her alone, Miguel. My clerks are off limits to you." I slammed the door and faced both of them. Flo looked ready to leap for his throat. Miguel was texting someone. I wanted to bash both of them in the head with something heavy to get their attention. Where was a weapon when I needed one?

FIVE

"Would you two pay attention? What *is* the plan?" I sat on the table I kept in the back room. Jerry and I had had some great times there. I needed to call Jer and tell him everything. I was the one who demanded communication in our relationship. Flo definitely shouldn't be keeping secrets from her husband either, especially not one this big and life-threatening.

"Glory, you are absolutely right." Miguel slid his phone into his back pocket. "Florence, you need to call Richard and get him involved in this."

"No." She sat in the only chair in the room and crossed her legs. After looking for a place to put it and finding nowhere she considered clean enough, she set her Chanel bag on her lap. "This is *my* problem. Ricardo has nothing to do with this."

"That's where you're wrong." Miguel sat on the table next to me, his leg against mine. Not for the first time, I wondered why there were absolutely no sparks between us. I slapped his hard thigh.

"Don't read my mind."

"You're too easy. Obviously you were thinking that Florence needs to tell her husband what's going on. You're right and I have the reason right here." Miguel's phone buzzed. "Let me answer this then I'll show you." He hopped down and answered. There was a muttered conversation, mostly monosyllables on his part. It was in a foreign language but I did hear Richard's name. That got Flo on her feet next to him, her hands fisted.

"What the hell have you done?" She was so upset she'd dropped her purse on my concrete floor and hadn't noticed. I jumped down and scooped it up. The expensive purse looked okay but I couldn't stand to see it lying there in harm's way.

"Relax, Florence, I'm working to save you. Obviously you heard both sides of my conversation. I have contacts all over Europe. The vampire on the phone lives near the town where the head of the Maury family has a chateau."

"And this vampire is on our side? What's this about my husband?" Flo realized her purse was missing and snatched it out of my hands. After a quick inspection, she set it on the chair.

Miguel laughed. "Darling, no one is on your side in this. These guys do favors to get favors in return. Saul is well-known and a good connection as you know. The Maurys are mortal but have plenty of money. No one cares about them but they have the sway an ancient name and money can buy. Or did until they picked on Saul."

"Yes, I knew it! The Maurys have made a *grande*

errore hurting him. But Ricardo! Tell me. I heard his name." Flo made the mistake of grabbing Miguel's jacket. His look could have melted steel. She stepped back and shook her fingers as if he'd singed them. "Say you can fix this, Cisneros."

"Maybe, maybe not, princess. If you weren't Glory's friend, I would have left you to your fate." Miguel looked her over with cold eyes. As usual Flo was dressed for success. Tonight she wore vintage Chanel head to toe. Her shoes were perfect leather pumps with a bow on the toe. Her suit was straight from the Grace Kelly era, pink and black. I didn't doubt she'd bought the entire ensemble new back in the day from CoCo herself. It would sell in the shop in a heartbeat and for big bucks. Princess was right.

"Miguel, don't say that. Okay, I know you're doing us both a favor. We appreciate it, don't we, Flo?" I nudged her and she smiled weakly.

"Yes, I do. Sorry if I do not seem grateful, *signore*. This is upsetting and when you say my husband's name…" She sniffled.

"Okay, enough with the mysterious looks. Tell us what's going on, Miguel." Forget Flo's exquisite taste. We had a bigger problem than what to wear to her funeral.

"I called in some favors, put out the word about the Maurys and the way they treated Saul. People don't like that. Now the Maury family is panicking, working the phones, calling in reinforcements. They can buy paranormals to take their side and this could turn into a war over there. Saul isn't stupid. That's bad for business. He wants to broker a peace." Miguel glanced down when his phone signaled a text.

"Why? They hurt Saul. He should want to see

them wiped off the face of the earth!" Flo stomped around the workroom, looking angry again. "He'd better not drag Ricardo into this."

"Saul is all about the bottom line, Princess. The Maury family has quite a few influential friends who do business with him as well. Saul plays both sides in this. Bones and bruises heal. He doesn't want to lose any customers, no matter how difficult they are." Miguel looked up from his phone, his glance at Flo saying what his words hadn't. Obviously my pal was one of Saul's more difficult clients.

"I won't give up the necklace." Flo's stubborn look could be used for billboards. It would make anyone pause to read the message, whatever it was.

"I get that, Florence. So does Saul. But he knows of something else the Maury family wants desperately. Apparently he and your husband had a conversation the last time you were in Saul's shop. Richard Mainwaring owns something that the family would take in trade. And they would call off the hit if they could get this rare item."

"But--"

"Wait, Flo. This sounds like a win. Doesn't Richard own thousands of ancient documents, artifacts, stuff like that? Maybe it's something that isn't that important to him." I slipped my hand around her shoulders. "Sit. Think for a minute. These people are making a concession. And should you really be keeping something this big a secret from Richard anyway?"

"I don't like it. Ricardo paid good money for the necklace. A deal is a deal." Flo wasn't softening. She glanced at Miguel. "Don't listen." She got up and pulled me with her into the bathroom. "Men do not need to know every little thing, Glory. You will find in your own marriage that it is necessary to protect Jeremiah from some truths that he would rather not know."

"Which is why I will never marry." Miguel said through the door. We could hear the click of the keys. He was texting again. "Should I tell them no deal? I can't promise the Maurys won't find another hit man to take my place once they figure out I'm not taking care of you."

I pulled Flo back out of the bathroom to give him a probing look. "You're not?"

Miguel held up his hand. "Quit trying to read my mind, Glory. I told you. I gave up wet work. I didn't take their money."

"Don't text them yet." I faced Flo so she could see I was serious. "I don't want to upset you, pal, but if you don't tell Richard now, I will. This is too important. If it means losing you as a friend, I'm sorry, but I can't stand the idea of you in danger or losing your life."

"Damn it, Glory." Flo's eyes filled. "You don't play fair." She muttered some Italian then pulled out her phone. This was a new one, the cover a brilliant blue with her initials etched in crystals. She hit speed dial then burst into tears. Silently she handed the phone to me.

"Florence? What the hell is going on? Are you crying?" Richard sounded frantic.

"It's Glory, Richard. We're at my shop and Flo has a confession to make to you. Can you come over?"

"It's about time. She's been blocking her thoughts every waking moment for weeks. I thought maybe she'd been on a shopping spree again and didn't want me to know. Is this more serious than that?" He sounded calm now.

"Afraid so. Better hurry." I ended the call.

"He will be so mad." Flo pulled out a linen hanky and wiped her eyes. Waterproof mascara. Of course she still looked beautiful. "He can forgive anything except lying. I have told some, what you call, whoppers lately. To keep him from knowing about this."

"He loves you. He'll forgive you but he'll be worried about you. Miguel, you have the details about this thing the Maurys want?" I wiped at my own tears. I hoped I was right. I knew Jerry hated to be left out of the loop on any kind of danger to me too. We'd gone round and round about that issue.

Miguel showed us a picture on his phone. "It's a religious thing. I just hope he really has this relic they want. Is Richard into that stuff?" The photo wasn't the best, but showed a box lined with red velvet. A glass tube was inside containing something small and brown nestled into a niche clearly made just for it. "It's supposed to be a piece of the True Cross, stolen from a reliquary somewhere. Legend says it has healing powers." Miguel looked up. "Apparently one of the older Maurys, the matriarch, is gravely ill. This makes me think this whole deal about the necklace has been a ploy to get to Richard's piece."

"Well, it won't work." Flo reached for the phone but Miguel wasn't giving it up. "I may have seen this before. Ricardo is very religious." Flo crossed herself. "Finding ancient artifacts is one of his passions. If this is that *importante* he will have it locked away and well guarded. Or have donated it back to the Church.

The True Cross. *Mio Dio*! Do you know how many people have come to Ricardo claiming they have such a thing?"

Miguel laughed. "Yeah, I've been researching that stuff. Why, the cross Jesus died on must have been fucking gigantic to have so many pieces!"

"Ai!" Flo began frantically crossing herself. "*Mio Dio*! Step back, Glory. The lightning will strike this man any moment." She backed up until she hit the wall then dropped her face into her hands.

"If I was going up in flames, it would have happened long before this." Miguel was still chuckling. Flo wasn't. Her shoulders heaved and I heard a sob.

"Flo, what is it?" I patted her shoulder. "Don't let Miguel's blasphemy bother you. Ignore him."

She looked up with welling eyes. "It's not him. If Ricardo thinks he has an actual relic of this value, so precious, I cannot... No! It is too much! I cannot ask him--"

"Ask him what?" Richard walked in from the shop, closing the door behind him. "What's going on, Florence? What in the hell is that criminal doing here?" He glared at Miguel then exclaimed when Flo threw herself into his arms. She sobbed against his dark blue sweater. "Answer me. Has he threatened you? Hurt you? By God!" His hate-filled look would have made most men run for the back door.

Miguel merely smiled but I saw him slide a slim piece of carved wood from a pocket inside his jacket. A stake. The sight of it made me step back behind Richard. Okay, so that was cowardly. But vampires and stakes don't mix.

"Relax, Richard. Miguel is helping her. He

brought us news that has saved her life. At least so far." I sucked it up and eased out to sit on the table again. Miguel held onto his smile but I knew him well enough by now to know he was wound up, ready to spring into action if Richard made a move toward him. Richard had his hands full with Flo weeping and mumbling against his shirt. He bent down to listen to her.

"That's insane. Saul sold us the necklace. Yes, he was reluctant but, when we agreed on the price, nothing was said about an owner having a previous claim."

"I know!" Flo leaned back. "It is so unfair, Ricardo. Can you believe they hired this man to kill me? Because I would not give them my beautiful necklace. I love it. I remember Marie wearing it. Such happy times before..." Tears ran down her cheeks. "Pah! Maybe it *is* bad luck. I should give it back anyway."

"I'm afraid it's too late for that to satisfy them now, Florence. Yes, they'd take it back, but they want something else too. You know what." Miguel passed me his phone.

"You're not giving back the necklace. What else are they asking for? Money? How much?" Richard stuck out his hand. "Show me."

I set the phone in his hand. "This. It's a religious relic. Apparently you own it."

"I don't believe it. How did they know I have it?" He practically threw the phone at Miguel. "Saul. Such a good friend to you, darling. He's not very discreet, is he?"

"I'm so sorry. This is all my fault." Flo studied his face. He was a handsome man with compelling blue eyes and white hair that made him unforgettable. Right now, I'd run like hell if I met him in a dark alley. His rigid jaw meant trouble for someone. "You're mad at me. I don't blame you. I am a greedy, selfish *cagna*."

"I would never call you a bitch, darling." He pulled her into his arms and kissed the top of her head. But I could see his eyes. They were cold, disappointed. This had affected him more than he wanted her to know.

"But you would call me selfish." Flo wasn't fooled. "I had to have the necklace and now it may cost you something dear to you."

"Not if I can help it. And I blame myself. I never should have mentioned the relic to Saul. It's just so rare. Such a great find." Richard bit his lip. "Shit. I couldn't resist bragging a little when Saul tried to sell me an ordinary piece pilfered from the Vatican stores."

Flo kissed his firm chin. "I'm so sorry. It is too bad of Saul to do this. We must find a way…"

"Yes, well, fill me in." Richard pushed Flo into the chair, not quite as gently as he usually handled her. "Cisneros, exactly what do these people think is going to happen?"

"That you'll give me the relic and I'll bring it to them." Miguel leaned against the back door. "You have something else in mind? I'd love to double cross these ignorant, greedy mortals."

"Yes, I think we can come up with a few tricks of our own." Richard smiled. "I don't like what you do."

"Did. I'm going legit. Glory is helping improve my image. We are," Miguel nodded to me, "friends. Right, Glory?"

"I guess. Though I can't for the life of me figure out why." And wasn't that the truth. There was something about this man that made me trust him and consider him my friend. Go figure. When he and Richard put their heads together to discuss strategies, I decided to leave them to it. I pulled a drained Flo over to the costumes I was considering and cheered her up with a decision making session.

It was almost laughable when we decided on a toga. My mother is a goddess on Olympus. Maybe I was taking a big chance dressing like her. I knew if I dared tell her about my wedding she'd go crazy. She hated the idea of my being a vampire. The only thing worse? For me to marry one.

"Okay, we have a plan. It will come together on the night of the Winter Solstice Ball. Good thing you got me that invitation, Glory." Miguel seemed to be in good spirits. Richard too. He even agreed to wear a costume to match Flo's Marie Antoinette. When I heard what they planned to do, I just swallowed. I was going to have to tell Jerry about it. Get him involved. If things fell apart, they'd need another strong vampire in their corner and no one was better equipped to help than my Jerry.

SIX

The week before the ball, Flo hosted a bridal shower that absolutely blew me away. It was at her house, a gorgeous contemporary home perched on a hilltop with views of Austin glittering below. It seemed like every female vampire and shifter in town had come bearing gifts. Flo had found a caterer, a former Energy Vampire who had gone into business making edible treats for vamps, and we grazed on chocolates that didn't upset our systems and other magical concoctions. The guy handed out business cards. I had a feeling Flo had worked out a deal with him to get a discount so that he could make good connections with local paranormals.

Jerry and Richard sat on the balcony smoking cigars and drinking some of the premium synthetic blood Flo had served in crystal goblets. I now had a dozen of those goblets too. When the last of the guests left, Flo and I stared at each other across the mounds of tissue paper and gift bags. I had luxurious bath towels, satiny sheets and even a set of fine china—in case I entertained some of my shifter friends. The dishes were from the girls who worked for me, the very shifters who hoped for an invitation to my new place. I knew they couldn't afford what they'd given me. Their gift wasn't the only one that had made me blink back tears. My friends had been way too generous. Flo had registered for me at all the major department stores and of course her taste was expensive.

"Flo, you are amazing. I can't believe you threw this party together in less than two weeks." I stroked the velvety towel on top of a stack. Fingertip? Hand towel? I didn't know or care. Everything was neutral because I'd never gotten around to picking colors.

"It was nothing. Now I have one more little gift. From me to you. For the honeymoon." Flo pulled a package from under the couch.

I recognized the wrapping from one of her favorite shops in Paris. It was an expensive boutique that sold lingerie. "No, you've done enough, Flo!"

"Don't be ridiculous. This is fun. I called and ordered this and they shipped it to me. I saw it the last time I was there and thought of you. This will be *perfetto* for your wedding night. Open it and see!" Her eyes were glittering and she clapped her hands. "I almost wish we could call the men in to see their reaction. Jeremiah's tongue will be hanging out. But I think if he sees it now, it might be unlucky."

"You are always worried about luck, aren't you? I bet this is naughty." I laughed and pulled off the top of the box. Inside was a sheer silk nightgown in glowing colors of blue and turquoise. Ribbons held up the lacy top and tied at the shoulders. "Oh, it's so beautiful and feminine!"

"I thought so. Black is predictable. No?" Flo touched the silk that hung from the bodice in stripes that reminded me of waves. I could see her hand through the fabric. "And red? Too harsh against the skin. This matches your eyes and will make your skin glow. It will remind Jeremiah that you were once a siren, a goddess who knows everything about lovemaking."

My hands shook as I carefully folded the gown and closed the lid. Yes, I'd been a siren once. But my memory of that had been wiped away. Thank God I couldn't remember my many years of calling men to me and killing them.

"Oh, I'm sorry. You look upset. You must forget I said that, Glory. Jeremiah is so in love with you, I know you must make him very happy in the bedroom. Am I right?" Flo sat next to me on her long forest green velvet couch and patted my back.

"Yes. We make each other happy. Because we love each other. This is a beautiful gift, Flo. Thank you for being my friend." I leaned against her. "In my long life, I've had few friendships that have lasted. You know what I mean."

"Yes, I do." She leaned too and we sat there a minute, connected, thinking back to the way a vampire's life made moving on a necessity. Changing names and losing mortals who we'd grown attached to was a sad fact of our life. Finally, we both sighed then laughed.

"Hey, enough of this. I'm starting a new chapter as Jerry's wife. No more moving on and leaving everyone I love behind. I swear it." I clinked my glass against Flo's and we drank every drop. Just in time, the caterer came in with fresh goblets of premium synthetic blood.

"I'm done now. Anything else, Ms. DaVinci?" He smiled at me. "Miss St. Clair, I'll be catering your wedding reception too. I hope that pleases you. Mr. Blade already talked to me about it."

"Yes, that's great. Everything here was perfect." I took a sip of the really nice A-B negative synthetic, my favorite. Once again I'd ignored details and Jerry had stepped in to handle the planning. It should bother me but instead I felt relieved. Was I an unnatural bride to let Flo then Jerry take the reins in this important event in my life? I refused to worry about that now. "Do you have that blood with the champagne kick?"

"Yes, of course. I'll make sure we serve that for the toast." He gathered up the last of the glasses and put them on his tray. "You have my card if you think of anything else you want specifically. I'll be coordinating with the mortals at the venue. Only two more weeks! I know you're excited." He grinned. "We'll have to do some major mind control out there but don't you worry about a thing. I've done it before. I hope this will be a first of many such events for me." He laughed. "A vampire wedding. You don't get many of those. What with the old ball and chain supposedly lasting forever."

"I think my husband has a check for you. He is outside. You see him?" Flo jumped up and practically shoved the man toward the patio doors. "Thank you. I am very pleased." She turned to me as soon as he was out with the door closed behind him. "Stop it. I see your face. You're not getting the cold feet, are you?"

I drained my glass, wishing Flo had gone with the champagne blood. There was a knot in my stomach the size of the fluffy silk comforter CiCi had given me. While it was as light as a feather, it looked at least three feet wide even folded.

"Worried? Me? And how could my feet get cold when I have on these great boots?" I held out one foot. I'd scored some vintage Ralph Lauren riding boots the week before and stuffed my black jeans into them.

Flo wasn't about to be distracted. "This is my fault. You have had my little problem on top of wedding plans to think about. And then there's your new apartment. When are you moving in?"

"Your problem is not little." I got up. "We've been really busy at the store, which is a good thing. And the apartment is almost ready. No furniture yet but we could move in this week if we settled for some of my old stuff and Jer's bedroom suite."

"I'm not hearing about your feelings about this wedding. Talk to me." Flo grabbed my hands. "I swear you turned even more pale than usual when that vampire talked about a ball and chain. Don't be scared to marry your lover. He makes you happy, doesn't he?"

"Of course he does!" I squeezed her fingers. "And Jerry's doing everything he can to make this perfect. Paying the freight for the wedding of the century when I'm pretty sure the bride's family is supposed to pick up the tab for that." I glanced up at the ceiling. "Okay, I admit I'm living in fear that my mother will show up any minute. You know she'll throw an Olympus-sized fit when she finds out I'm marrying a vampire. She hates anyone with fangs."

"Of course Jeremiah will pay. He can afford it. And forget your mother." Flo's gesture toward the ceiling was obviously the Italian version of a kiss-off. "If your mama does show up, we ignore her. It's way too late for her to interfere in your business." Flo pulled me toward the patio doors. "Remember. You are in love. Jeremiah worships you. He is your soulmate. Do you want to let him go?"

"No, of course not." I stopped her before she could open the French door. "But this is suddenly moving so fast. In less than two weeks…"

"He will be yours. All yours." Flo hugged me. "You are so lucky to have found each other. Think about how many women never meet the man they are destined for."

I stood in the circle of her arms and let that thought soak in. She was so right that it helped me push down my nerves. I nodded. "Thanks. I'm off the ledge now."

"I don't know what you mean, but I like your smile. Now let's get the men and load your treasures into Jeremiah's big car. For once I am glad these men like their SUBs. He can carry all of this to your new place in one trip."

"Right. And I'm ordering furniture tomorrow night. Everything new. For the first time in my life." I heard myself giggle. Well, excuse me, but after hundreds of years of penny pinching it was cool to get to throw money around. Too bad there was still that nagging little voice inside me insisting that things were too good to be true. Glory St. Clair didn't deserve a brand new life with a man who adored her.

And no money worries? Something was going to go wrong. Guaranteed.

It took six trips to Jerry's car to load all the wonderful gifts and then we were on our way. Jerry kept his hand on my leg during the drive to Sixth Street, obviously content that things were moving right along. He seemed confident that even the showdown he and Richard were planning with Miguel at the Winter Solstice Ball next week would go off without a hitch. I just smiled and pretended I was on the same page as he drove us downtown. But after dragging pile after pile of gifts up to the second floor and our apartment that smelled of fresh paint and the future, I knew I was due for a meltdown.

"Okay, there's something wrong. I know you. Look at all these presents. Your friends are generous. You should be happy. Instead you're sitting there brooding. What's on your mind?" Jerry sat on the floor across from me.

He was right. We'd dumped the loot in the middle of our empty living room floor. All except the dishes and glassware. Oh, excuse me. Crystal. That was in the kitchen on the granite countertop. Flo insisted I should line my shelves with some sort of paper before I put that stuff away. Shelf paper? I couldn't imagine. So the boxes were on the black granite. Jerry's pick. Dramatic. I admit I liked it.

"Check out this loot as you called it in the car. Notice anything?" I nudged a pile of towels with my bare foot. I'd left my boots at the door. The wood floor had just been laid and I dreaded the first scratch. It certainly wouldn't be from one of my heels.

Jerry picked up a towel and rubbed it on his

cheek. "Nice. Soft. Lots of them. Similar colors so we won't have to worry about mixing them up, I guess. They go with the tile in either bathroom."

"Yes, exactly." I looked around. Off white walls. I didn't have to get up to know that every finish in the apartment was neutral—beige, off white, stone, whatever. Damian had come by the night before and gone on long and loud about resale values, approving all the choices as perfect if we decided to move on and look for a buyer.

"You hate this place." Jerry leaned back on both hands, his legs out in front of him. "Why didn't you say something? You could have picked out the colors, finishes. No, you said, go ahead, do whatever you want. First it was that you were busy with the shop and then it was the wedding. Finally you ended up getting involved in Flo's mess."

"I don't hate this place." I scooted next to him and threw my arms around him, my head on his shoulder. "It's big, bright, and the closets are enormous. A dream come true." I sighed, frustrated with myself for letting things slide. When had I lost control? Or had I ever had it in the first place? It seemed like once I set a date, some kind of momentum had taken over and here we were. "But look at this stuff they gave me. Jer. Ecru, beige, stone, wheat, ivory, cream, desert sand, khaki…" I rolled off of him and fell back to lay staring at the ceiling. "I could go on and on."

He leaned over me. "And what's the problem again?"

"They aren't colors, Jer. They're, uh, neutral!" I sat up, almost hitting him in the nose. "Am I neutral? Am I?" I heard my voice rising but couldn't stop.

"Look at me." Okay so I had on my usual black pants, but my top was a brilliant raspberry vee-neck. "Do I try to blend into the woodwork?" I glanced at the walls and wood trim, "Which in here is a color no doubt called Tuscan white."

"Well excuse me for going with the logical choice." Jerry laughed and wrestled me to the floor until he was on top of me, our body parts fitting together in a most logical way that got me immediately distracted. "No, my love, you are not neutral, which you seem to equate with boring. You want to paint the walls purple? Have at it. Take this stuff back and exchange it for bright colors? I say go for it. When our friends come we can bring out a token hand towel in boring beige. Does that make you happy?" He slid one hand under me, pulling me tight against him.

"Well, yes." I knew I was acting the fool, but I didn't care. Call it nerves or whatever, this road to domestic bliss had seemed headed to Jerry Land. It had to have my stamp on it somewhere or I was very afraid I'd lose myself. Become Mrs. Jerry not Glory at all anymore.

"Then that's what we'll do." He reached behind him and grabbed one of the decorative bags covered in wedding bells. It was full of king-sized sheets. "Look, there's a gift receipt in the bottom of this bag. It tells where this set was purchased. Now I'm very interested in what color sheets you favor for our bed. Not those awful pink flowered things Richard complains about I hope." He leaned down to nip my earlobe then ran his lips to my jugular. "What about a dark red, the color of your blood?"

"That seems a little, mmm, yes, bite me there,

Jer," I sighed when he did. "too vampirish. I look good in blue. Blue sheets. Or green. Though that sounds predictable."

"Can't have that." Jerry laughed, going to work on my pants. "Gloriana, you know you're driving me mad, don't you? First because you are too busy to help with the apartment and now... Oh, hell, just keep surprising me."

"I will." I wiggled out of my pants, glad to help him change the subject to something much more interesting. "Animal print." I slid my hands under his shirt. "To bring out the beast in you."

"Do we need sheets for that?" He growled and dragged a soft pillow under my butt.

"We should go shopping together." I grinned when he groaned and leaned back.

"Now you're threatening me. On-line shopping? Maybe. I've got the wi-fi already set up. And I bought you something to go with it. A shower gift. Wait here."

"You're leaving me here, on the floor half naked and ready to play?" I couldn't believe it.

"Patience, love. I think you'll like this. And we have a lifetime to explore this apartment together, naked and otherwise." He tossed his shirt aside as he walked away. I had to admire his broad shoulders and the way his jeans hugged his firm butt. I couldn't wait to strip them off.

A gift? I lay back, beginning to see a pattern. Jerry was going to keep buying me things and I was going to have to get used to living the pampered life of a rich vampire. It was Monday and my shop was closed. I was a lady of leisure. So maybe I should relax and just enjoy the thought of a future drinking premium synthetics and not worrying about rent. He was back in moments with a case that I recognized, though this one was hot pink. I sat up.

"What have you done?" I kept my hands in my lap though I wanted to reach out and snatch that case.

"I can't stand to watch you struggle with your ancient laptop another night. So I bought you a new tablet. Not a very romantic gift, I know. Flo thought I should buy you jewelry. But Richard helped me pick this out. He installed all the software and--"

"I love it!" I grabbed it before he could say another word. "I love *you*!" I pulled him in for a deep kiss then practically tossed him aside so I could open the case and check out my new toy. I had pride, sure I did. But I'm not stupid. Flo could keep her jewelry. My guy knew me. This could help in my business. I recognized my favorite programs and bookmarks. Richard must have borrowed my laptop when Flo and I were out shopping and downloaded everything I liked. I opened a shopping site.

"Okay, lover, come here and pick out new sheets." I grinned when Jerry groaned. "Kidding." I gently set the tablet aside. "Come here and let me show you how much I love your idea of a perfect gift." I stripped off my sweater and threw it aside.

"Now you're talking." He growled again and launched himself at me.

#

The Winter Solstice Ball. I felt free and easy in my long white toga. The evening was relatively mild and my sleeveless gown hugged my curves in a way that had Jerry sticking close. He'd pleased Flo when he'd bought me a diamond pin to place on my shoulder. It was a bat, which made me giggle. When my mother donned a toga, she always wore a diamond pin but it certainly wasn't anything that could possibly be related to vampires. Looking at Flo in her fancy and very difficult to wear Marie Antoinette gown and Diana Marchand in her Scarlett O'Hara Southern belle costume, I was very happy with my choice. There were plenty of other women dressed in fancy gowns, along with flappers, Egyptian queens and even a mermaid. That was Lacy who had come with Rafe. I was a little surprised to see him there but apparently he was a good customer of Damian's.

"I hope you're having a good time." Damian, our host, had gone for the swashbuckling look, a masked pirate complete with ruffled shirt. I had a feeling the sword he wore was the real thing. He'd tried to get everyone to wear masks and some had gone along with the idea. Jerry wouldn't allow it, too into defense for the upcoming showdown with the Maurys.

Damian and Miguel had hit it off and their talk of a fencing club had moved forward. It was the talk of the ball. There were several men wearing swords, even a trio dressed as Musketeers. Jerry and Richard were interested in joining the club too. Ancient vamps did like their swordplay.

"You aren't dancing. Gloriana, you won't let him waste this music, will you?" Damian grinned, obviously loving his role as host.

"Of course not." I held Jerry's hand. "You know how I love to dance."

"Not sure we have time for that. Any sign of the enemy?" Jerry glanced around almost eagerly. He looked delicious in his Campbell plaid. He certainly had the legs for it. We'd had to bring Damian in on our plans for the Maury situation. After all, the showdown was going to be at his party.

"My security detail hasn't reported any problems. There are a few mortals that are invited guests, so the intruders could slip in with them. I'll let you know if I hear anything." Damian looked me over. "Ah, Gloriana, you are very goddess-like tonight. Beautiful. I think you and I should tango together."

"I think not." I winked. "I'm sticking with my fiancé tonight. He and I'll tango if I decide to dance one."

Jerry groaned. "You know I can't do those kinds of fancy steps. Go with my blessing. Damian knows I'd carve out his heart if he makes a fool's move on you."

"Well, then. Come get me if they play one, Damian." I laughed. "Really, Jer. The tango is the dance of love." I bumped him with my hip. "And, darling, you have leaped over swords with bagpipes playing. So that excuse isn't working for me."

Damian pulled my hand to his lips. "And we'd see if you could carve out my heart or if I did yours." He dropped my hand. "Later, Gloriana." He strode away.

"My brother. You'd think we were just here to have a good time." Flo sashayed up to us. Her sapphire necklace looked fiery in the light from the candles that blazed around the edge of the outdoor dance floor. Richard stood close to her, his hand on her elbow. He had on a courtly French costume, his sword strapped on as well. Neither of them wore a mask.

"We are, darling. Relax. We have this well in hand." He smiled at us. "You left the broadsword at home, Jeremiah."

"Gloriana put her foot down. And I have to admit it would have torn the upholstery in the car." Jerry gave me an accusing look.

"Exactly. And you wouldn't have been able to dance with it strapped on either." I grabbed his hand. "Here's a nice slow one. Come on." I nodded to Flo. "You've got lots of friends here. We're watching."

"I know. Have fun. I am in a bad mood. Ignore me." She turned to Richard. "We dance too. It is the best way to pass the time."

"Of course." He pulled her into his arms, her skirt belling out behind her. "Cisneros is here. See him by the band? Looks like he's talking to Israel Caine. Surely he wouldn't involve him in our problem."

"I doubt it. But he and Ray get along all right ever since Miguel arranged for Aggie, the former Siren, to go out to L.A. and work with the record label there. Ray was glad to see the last of her." I threw this over my shoulder right before Jerry danced me away from the pair.

"You and Cisneros. I'm still not sold on what you insist is a friendship. You have too damned many male friends." Jerry held me close, his chest hard against my breasts. The fact that I could feel a knife against my waist wasn't exactly a turn-on.

I bit back a grin. "What can I say? Men like me. You know there's nothing else to it." I looked up at my lover. It had taken lots of fast talking to get Jerry to agree to have anything to do with Miguel. The fact that the hit man had warned Flo instead of taking the contract had gone a long way toward convincing him that Miguel was a necessary evil here. Also, Richard was on board. Jerry and Richard's friendship was solid. They'd spent hours discussing what they expected to happen tonight. "No one lights my fire but you, Jerry."

"I know that." His confident smile came from knowing he'd made me scream my pleasure just an hour before, as we were getting ready to come to the ball. "I'm not jealous, Gloriana. But this meeting tonight may not go as smoothly as we hope. I'd like you to stay away from Cisneros, Florence, and Richard until we get this deal settled tonight." Jerry scanned the dance floor, on alert. He was ever the warrior, though it was easy to forget it when he wasn't in his plaid. Tonight he looked the part with that dangerous looking knife stuck in his wide leather belt.

"Now why are you trying to spoil this evening by bossing me around? You know that doesn't work with me." I pinched his hand. "Even though you have made me very happy lately."

He shrugged and looked into my eyes. "I had to give it a try. You are one stubborn wench. You know that, right?"

"Which is just one reason you love me. See anything significant?" I looked around when he twirled me. Miguel was dressed in his Rhett Butler garb. He now stood next to Diana Marchand. I was right, his Southern look charmed her and she was fluttering her fan at him. But I wasn't fooled. He was giving her only half of his attention. The rest was on the open doors that led from the house. He suddenly gave Diana a courtly bow and moved quickly toward them.

"A group of three men just came out of the house. They're dressed in cowboy costumes if you can believe it. I have a feeling they thought they'd blend in, being in Texas and all." Jerry grinned. I knew he was itching for a fight. "I smell mortals." His hand left my waist to slide down to his knife.

"Relax, Jer. You're supposed to negotiate, trick these people, and not make this into a battle royal."

"But I love battles. It's been way too long." He dropped my hand and I realized the song had ended.

"Ladies and gentlemen, may I have your attention? I've asked one of my guests to sing for us and he had a great idea. Israel Caine, come up here." Damian waved to Ray who strode to the microphone in front of the band. "If any of you were at N-V on Halloween night, you heard our own Gloriana St. Clair sing for the first time in public. She did a great job and sang a duet with Ray here. Glory, would you mind coming up and taking the mic with Ray for an encore performance?" Damian began clapping and the audience joined in.

I looked for Miguel, pretty sure this was on him, but he'd disappeared. Had he and Jerry arranged to get me out of the way so they could handle the Maury confrontation without me? Damian stopped in front of me and held out his hand. Ray was saying something into the microphone about our song choices Halloween night. I realized I couldn't say no. I had too many friends here and Jerry was practically shoving me at Damian. I let the Italian lead me to the podium.

"This is a surprise. We haven't rehearsed so forgive us if we're a little rusty." I turned off the mic and whispered to Ray. His eyes lit up and he laughed. Oh, yes, he was happy to stick it to anyone who tried to tell me what to do, especially Jerry. He turned and talked to the band. Luckily it was a popular song they knew and they shifted to a key we were both comfortable with. As soon as the audience heard the opening bars, cheers went up. We were ready to rock.

We sang "A Crazy Little Thing Called Love." It was a Queen classic and had a great beat. It certainly gave Ray and me a chance to play off of each other. Every eye was on us. It wasn't a hot ballad so I knew it wouldn't make Jerry or Ray think there was anything real going on between the rocker and me. It was just a fun, upbeat tune that let us show off our singing chops. The message was clear though—my lover should be "cool" and "relax." At the end Ray and I fell into each other's arms, both of us pumped by the song and the roar of the crowd. They wanted an encore but I bowed to Ray, letting him take a solo turn while I waved and disappeared off the stage, looking for Jer and the rest of the crew.

But they were gone. All of them. Oh, no, I wasn't letting them get away with that. I used my vamp senses and got a whiff of mortal, following my nose to the edge of this property that sat on a hilltop. Damian had bought the acreage close to downtown Austin for three reasons: the spectacular view of the city, the fact that it came with a castle built by an eccentric millionaire back in the day and that it was surrounded by an electrified security fence. The three mortals surrounded by three angry vampires looked like they were ready to take their chances with the fence and the steep drop on the other side when I arrived. Flo landed next to me as I started to ease closer to hear what was going on.

SEVEN

Richard had his sword tip pressed against one mortal's chest, about where his heart should be. "You want to explain what in the hell is going on?"

"I am Stefan Maury, these are my cousins. We're here to make a deal. You know the terms." The man held out his hands to show they were empty. They were steady, which was surprising considering the position he was in. "I have other men here who will make you sorry if you decide to break faith with us now." He nodded and I was suddenly grabbed from behind.

Flo shrieked and began to struggle. She was also being held by a burly vampire. How he'd gotten past security was anyone's guess. I tried to look into the man's eyes but he must have heard that there were vampires with special powers here and he wouldn't look at me. The guy behind me was really strong too and there was no way I could freeze him without eye contact.

"What the--" Jerry whirled, his knife in his hand.

"Don't try it. I have a stake close to her heart. She'll be gone before you can toss that blade," the man at my back said gruffly. Sure enough I felt a prick against the back of my toga. The smell of fresh blood filled the air.

"Same here, Mainwaring. If I push this stake in a few more inches, your wife is dead."

"Let them go." Miguel had managed to get behind the Maurys. Sparks flew when he tossed two of the men against the fence. They slumped, obviously shocked into silence. Now he held a knife against Stefan Maury's throat. "Is this worth your own life?"

"I can't go back without the relic. Keep the necklace. We don't care about it. But my grandmother is dying. She needs the True Cross. The priests in her village insist it will save her." The man had nerves of steel. He didn't flinch when Miguel drew a line across his cheek with the tip of his knife.

"And if she dies anyway? What then?" Miguel nodded to Jerry and Richard. They were staring at Flo and me, obviously looking for a way to get us free.

"Jerry, don't try anything. He's not bluffing. There really is a stake against my back. I can feel it."

"She's right, Ricardo. I'm so sorry." Flo sobbed. "But you must give him your relic."

"Of course, darling. But will they let you go then? How can I trust them?" Richard pulled a velvet box from inside his doublet.

"We need proof, of course. Of their good intentions." Miguel drew another bloody line on

Stefan's face. "I can smell Glory's blood from here. Let her go and I'll consider that a sign of good faith. Push her over here. You'll still have Florence as leverage."

"Very well. Let the blond go." Stefan bled from several cuts now but still stood straight and tall. That took a lot of courage considering the vampires surrounding him all had fangs down, his mortal blood doing a number on us.

The vampire holding me shoved me toward Jerry. I stumbled then turned and caught my captor's eyes. He was turned to stone before he could move another step. Then I jerked Flo free from the man who'd captured her, using the element of surprise to turn him into a statue as well.

"Seems like this fight is over." Damian ran up, his sword drawn. He nudged both of the frozen men with the tip, grinning when he realized they couldn't fight back. "Too bad. I have an itch to skewer one or both of them for making fools of my guards." Then he noticed Flo was bleeding, her gown stained as she sobbed in Richard's arms. "*Bastardo!* You hurt my sister?" He turned to me. "Only one person can freeze men in their tracks like this. Thaw them, Glory. I want a fair fight so I can kill them, one at a time." He slashed each man with his sword, making them bleed.

"No. Let them be. I can't stand to see you fight." Flo held out a hand to her brother. Damian ran to her and began exclaiming in Italian.

"Can we finish what we started here?" Miguel still held Stefan Maury close to the fence. His mortal friends were stirring, the electrical shock obviously not enough to kill them.

"Yes, let's finish it." Richard handed Flo over to Damian. "Listen to me, you piece of shit, don't you ever come after my family again. Do you hear me?"

"I can't promise that, *monsieur*. Kill me if you must, but I can't go home without the relic. You don't know my *grand-mère*." Stefan stared straight ahead. "She leads the family. I was given this task and, if I fail, I will suffer such as hell would be a welcome release."

I pulled away from Jerry who'd been holding me while he carefully examined the insignificant cut on my back from the stake.

"Wait. I know what it's like to have a difficult, um, relative. In my case it's my mother. Can't you at least let him borrow the relic, Richard?" Flo's husband still gripped it. He looked incredulous. "Come on. You know how to get it back if the old lady dies."

Stefan eyes, glazed with pain, focused on me. "You would plead my case? Yes, yes, of course I will make sure you get your relic back, Mainwaring, if *Grand-mère* dies. And if she lives, I will see that it finds its way back to you as well, even if I must risk my life to do it. *Grand-mère* will understand that you must treasure it. This illness has brought her closer to God." He rolled his eyes. "I'm sure God was surprised. Anyway, I can persuade her that this was a generous loan. That you are a pious man and due a handsome reward for it."

Richard and Flo stared at me. They whispered together then Flo took the velvet box from Richard. "Here, take it." She pushed it into Stefan's hands. "Perhaps you should hope it does not work miracles, eh? I keep the necklace. It is important to me. Do not bother me about it again. *Tu mi capisci?*"

"Yes, I understand. I can't thank you enough." Stefan swallowed. "Are you through carving your initials into my face, Cisneros?"

"Maybe, maybe not. For your information, I am out of the assassination business. Though I will certainly keep your money because of the trouble this has caused me and my friends here. Tell your people and the rest of your connections in Europe that Miguel Cisneros no longer takes hits." Miguel wiped off his blade on Stefan's cowboy shirt and slipped it out of sight. "And if I hear you've been bragging that you bested the Austin vampires to get this relic, I'll make sure the Maury family, every one of you, is wiped off the map. Do you believe me?"

"Yes, I do." Stefan tucked the velvet box into his jeans pocket and helped his cousins to their feet. "I will let you know how this turns out for my grandmother. Thank you, Mainwaring, Madame." He bowed toward Florence. "I am not sure I would have been as forgiving as you have been." He tipped his cowboy hat at the rest of us then marched out of sight, his two mortal friends staggering after him.

"Uh, what about them?" Flo pointed at the bleeding vampires who were still frozen in place.

"I'll take care of them. Gloriana isn't the only vampire who can pull that particular trick." That comment from Miguel raised eyebrows all around. "They are exceptionally nasty hired guns, but they only do what they are paid to do." He glanced around the group. "You never know when you might need someone like that. Leave them to me."

"Okay, Miguel, but make sure they leave town." I walked over and jerked the stakes out of each of their hands and tossed them over the electrified fence. We could hear the wood hit the rocks down below the steep cliff on the other side. "I don't want to be around when you do thaw them."

"Fine. I know how to handle their kind. They can hear us so they know this job is over. They'd better catch Stefan Maury if they want to be paid. After the party is over. You agree, Sabatini?" Miguel nudged one of the men with his foot and, satisfied that he was still immobile, nodded at Damian.

"Yes, that's good. Now I say we all need a drink. The blood on the costumes is unfortunate. If either of you ladies would like to change, I have some silk robes upstairs…" Flo and I frowned. "Never mind. Of course other vampires may think the blood a nice touch, a charming decoration." Damian seemed to realize his joke was falling flat and shook his head. "Pah! Look on the bright side. We have the longest night of the year ahead of us to dance, drink and make love. I, for one, plan to enjoy it." He gestured toward where we could hear the band still playing, always the perfect host. "Come, the music is great and Gloriana has promised me a tango." He grinned and led the way.

I held onto Jerry and walked toward the music. A tango? I could barely stay on my feet. I'd come close to being staked and I'd never forget the feel of that wood against my skin. The wound still itched, the allergy we all had to a certain type of timber assuring me that it really could have killed me if it had hit my heart. I was always worried about how to spend eternity. Well, I'd just had a reminder that there were no guarantees that I'd live forever, none at all.

\#

It was Christmas night and we were finally moving into our new apartment. Jerry had let me order the furniture and he'd paid extra to get everything delivered on Christmas Eve. I hadn't been to the place since before the Winter Solstice Ball. Business at the shop had been crazy in a good way. I'd helped the clerks and been on a buying spree, contacting vamps I knew who liked to sell their vintage pieces so I could restock. I needed fresh merchandise for our emptying racks and shelves. I was actually getting over my bridal nerves and looking forward to becoming Jerry's wife. Imagine that.

"All right. I know we're not married yet but Florence said I have to carry you over the threshold anyway. For luck. She seems big on these kinds of things." Jerry lifted me into his arms as soon as we got to the top of the stairs. We had a new door, a shiny red one with a peephole so I could see who was on the other side before I opened it. Not that my vamp senses didn't usually tell me anyway.

"This is new. Wasn't the other one just solid dark wood?" I leaned down to turn the brass knob.

"Yes, but I've made a few changes since you were here last." He kissed me long and hard then set me on my feet in the small tile entryway. "Surprise!"

"I can't believe it!" I gazed around me. The walls in the entry were a pale turquoise. When we stepped into the spacious living room the color deepened to the blue of the Mediterranean. The white leather couch I'd picked had a half-dozen colorful pillows scattered across it and a pair of print chairs matched perfectly.

"I hope you like it. I told the decorator I wanted the color of the water off the Amalfi coast.

Remember the trip we took there? I'll never forget how you looked on that beach, the water matching your eyes when a moonbeam hit them." He brushed my hair back from my face. "It was one of our perfect nights together."

"Jerry." I kissed him hard, so moved I struggled not to cry. "This is a romantic side you rarely show me. I remember that night. I was afraid to swim but you carried me into the waves and we made love there." I held onto him, remembering. How long ago had it been? Fifty years? Sixty? So many memories. I drew back. "You hired a decorator? When?"

"After you let me know how you felt about neutrals. Look around. You'll find that there's not one white wall left in this place. Come see our bedroom." He grinned and dragged me down the hall. "You can change anything you don't like, but it was easier to repaint when the place was empty."

I caught a glimpse of a terracotta kitchen with splashes of yellow and blue. The dining room was tricked out in emerald green that complimented the dark wood round table that would probably never see a dinner, just the poker parties Jerry had already warned me he wanted to throw there.

"What do you think?" He threw open the bedroom door like a magician showing off a great trick. I gasped.

"Wow!" I laughed and threw myself into the middle of the king-sized bed. He hadn't moved his bedroom suite here after all, but had ordered another set, this one with the kind of vintage look I loved. The massive French baroque headboard rose toward the ceiling and had been gilded, a mirror in its center. Too bad that mirror was wasted on us.

The walls were done in Venetian plaster, the deep peach a color that would make my skin glow in dim lighting. I was tempted to strip off right then to test the theory. The bedspread was sumptuous velvet, a royal blue with gold woven bee designs that I recognized from that period. Against one wall was a Venetian painted dressing table loaded with crystal perfume bottles. I couldn't resist hopping up to check them out. Gorgeous.

"Are you crazy? Are we going to be able to sleep in a room like this?" I lunged at Jerry, hugging him so hard I was afraid I'd cracked a rib. I should have known better. My man was warrior strong.

"We don't sleep. We die at sunrise, my love. And I hope you like it. The decorator was CiCi. She has pretty feminine taste. Has she pleased you?" Jerry glanced around the room. "She did finally put in a sturdy desk so both of us could use our computers. But she wouldn't allow a TV in here. Said I'd have to watch it in my Man Cave as she dubbed it. Come see. It's in one of the extra bedrooms." He dragged me out of our bedroom but only after I got a look at the master bath, resplendent with navy and gold towels and a dark furry rug that begged to be christened with a sexy romp.

"Man Cave? I may want to use this room too." I had to admit the deep red walls were amazing. The glaze glowed under the lights from a black iron chandelier that CiCi might have found in an old saloon. There was a vintage humidor for Jerry's cigars and a hidden TV that popped up when he pushed a remote. He played with his technology, showing off the stereo system and the way his leather chair vibrated with the touch of a button. I was more interested in the couch with a faux fur throw where both of us could snuggle to watch TV or DVDs.

"So can you live here with me? Happily ever after?" Jerry pulled me down to the couch. "Be honest. Paint is an easy thing to change."

"I love every bit of it." I sighed against him. "I can't wait to marry you. I'm beginning to wonder why I kept putting you off."

"I'm sure not going to remind you." He jumped up. "I hear the truck coming. They've got the last of the boxes and our clothes. Just wait here. I'll supervise the unloading. When it's done, I want us to start working our way through every room in the new place. You decide which room we're going to do first." He leaned down and kissed me gently, his palm cupping my breast. "You know exactly what I mean, don't you?"

"Yes, indeed." I ran a finger down his zipper, his jeans taut against his bulge. "Hurry them along." I grinned as he practically ran out of sight.

"Seems like I got here just in time."

I knew that voice. Had hoped to avoid it until after New Year's Day.

"Mother." I swallowed and stood. "What do you think of my new apartment?"

"It's beautiful. But you can't distract me with a tour of this place. Tell me you're not marrying that fanged monster." With her typical drama, my mother staggered over to Jerry's pride and joy, his new leather chair. It was a shame that we looked so much alike. She even appeared almost the same age as I did, though maybe closer to thirty than the twenty-two I'd been when I'd been made vampire. We had the same blond hair and blue eyes, the same figure though mine was more generous thanks to an eating binge and bloating right before I was turned.

We shared the same love of great clothes and shoes too. Mother hadn't come down in her toga tonight. No, she loved to rub in her knack for creating her own wardrobe with a magical blink. This visit she wore a Pucci print shift from the sixties and black ballet flats.

"He's not a monster, Mother, he's the love of my life. And if he *is* a monster, what does that make me?" I was not about to stand for criticism from her tonight, not of Jerry. He'd been nothing but wonderful lately.

"Misguided. Brainwashed. Take your pick." She sighed, pretending to be long-suffering.

"I pick happy." Maybe the devil made me do it, but I couldn't resist. I grabbed the remote and treated her to the massage button on high.

She shrieked and jumped out of the chair. "That man ruined your life. Can't you see it, Gloriana?"

"He gave me immortality. I would be dust by now if he hadn't turned me in 1604 and don't you forget it. But this is an old argument and I don't see the point. Be happy for me, Mother. If you love me like you say you do, you'll back off and let me live my life as I choose." I tossed aside the remote and strode to my new bedroom where I picked up one of the beautiful perfume bottles. No scent in it of course. Vampires rely on their sense of smell for defense and don't muddle it by using perfume. But I do love old crystal bottles. Bless CiCi for knowing that. I tensed when I felt Mother's hand on my shoulder.

"Darling. Of course I love you. But how can you think this is best for you? Drinking blood." She

94

turned me to face her just in time for me to see her shudder. "I can't bear the thought."

"I'm sorry, but I'm not changing." I realized I was about to crush the bottle or throw it against the wall so I gently set it down. "Look around. Jerry had this space decorated to please me. He treats me like a queen. I am happier than I've ever been in my life."

She reached past me and picked up a sterling frame from the dressing table. "So you've agreed to marry him?" Her voice rose several octaves. "This is a wedding invitation. You've planned a wedding for New Year's Day, less than a week away. Where's *my* invitation?"

"Where would I send it, Mother? Do you have a post office box on Olympus?" I snatched it out of her hand. CiCi had framed one of our invitations. It was a sweet gesture but now I had to deal with what was sure to be a scene.

"So am I invited?" She strode around the room, stroking the velvet coverlet, frowning down at the chaise lounge in the corner where CiCi had left one of my favorite self-help books. This one was about taking control of your life. Of course my mother wouldn't approve of that, *she* wanted to pull my strings.

"I'd love for you to be there if you can promise to be happy for me and not ruin my special night." I heard the front door opening. "Here's Jerry now. The movers are bringing in our clothes. Will you stay and be nice to him? Wish him, us, well?"

"You ask too much." She whirled to face me, her face a solemn mask. "I have plans for you, Gloriana, and they don't include a husband from this earthly plane. Especially not one who is a bloodsucker."

"Mother, you came to my life too late. I make my own plans." I knew I was taking a chance, defying her. But she'd abandoned me when I was a baby. Left me to be raised a Siren, in the Olympus version of an orphanage, to basically become a murdering prostitute. Can you blame me if I wasn't exactly eager to jump to do her bidding?

"We are not done, Gloriana. Not at all." And with that, she disappeared.

Jerry strode into the room with a box in his hands, followed by workmen carrying cardboard wardrobes that I knew were filled with my clothes and his. "Tell them where you want your things, Gloriana. We've got two more trips downstairs and then we're finished."

I found a smile and got busy. No way was I destroying Jerry's happy mood by sharing my mother's visit. But she was so powerful. If she had plans, I was sure they weren't to just stand by and let me marry the man I loved. I swallowed a sick feeling as I went through the motions necessary to put away my meager wardrobe in my fabulous new closet. I had built-in shelves for shoes and handbags, drawers for my lingerie. Stepping back and seeing my things looking so pretty was almost enough to help me forget...

"Come out here, Gloriana. I have one more gift for you. It *is* Christmas, you know." Jerry was acting like an excited kid. It had taken him all of ten minutes to stuff his underwear and socks into drawers. He'd told the men to hang his things wherever in *his* closet. Yes, he had his own on the other side of our master bath. Have I mentioned how much I love this apartment?

"Jerry, you've done enough." I dragged myself out of my walk-in, casting one more admiring look at the way I'd arranged everything by color. It probably wouldn't stay that way, but for now it was perfect. "I love, love, love everything here."

"One more thing. In this box." He gestured to the gold wrapped box sitting on the foot of our bed. It had a fluffy bow on top made of gold and silver ribbon. "Florence mentioned that you love these things and I asked Lacy to help me shop for it. I hope I got it right."

I knew from the size of the box that it probably wasn't jewelry. Which was good. Unlike my best bud, I really didn't wear much. A fur? I hoped not. Austin isn't exactly against fur, but isn't for it either. And we did have those mild winters.

"Would you just open it?" Jerry slid his arms around me. "The suspense is killing me. I don't buy stuff like this. And to order it on-line... I probably screwed it up."

"Okay, okay, but whatever it is, I'm sure I'll love it." I turned in his arms and kissed him, slowly, thoroughly. "Because you were thinking about what would please me. And I know what will please *you*. Maybe I'll get out the nightgown Flo gave me. It's supposed to be for our wedding night but this first night in our new place seems to be the right time. I think you'll find it stimulating." I teased one of his ears and saw him shiver.

"Quit stalling and get to it, woman. And you know I like you best in nothing at all." He pinched my butt and turned me around. He really nervous.

"Right." I took a breath and pulled open the box

top. "Oh, Jerry. I can't believe…" I pulled out the two-piece Chanel suit. It was the kind I'd always lusted after. Vintage. Couturier. Perfect in black with gold buttons and a little chain across the pocket. I held it up and knew it would fit.

"Flo said you have a thing for that designer. Lacy too. And she knew your size. She wouldn't tell me what *that* was. She gave me three options to choose from on the Internet." He studied my face. "This one seemed right. I know you like black and… Shit. Tell me if it's not to your liking." He sat on the bed next to the box.

I hugged the knit to me, actually speechless for a moment. "To my liking?" My voice shook. "Jerry, you have no idea. For years I've watched women wear these kinds of designer originals and wished…" I blinked. Yep, he'd made me cry. "I could never afford a piece like this. Never. Not even used. Because if I did run across a couturier vintage piece it was either too small or I had to sell it to support the store."

"Gloriana." Jerry took the suit from me and pulled me into his lap. "You will never have to sell something to survive again. I promise you that. I know you are an independent woman. I respect that. But it is my greatest wish that you will let me do this for you. I will always provide for you. Anything you want." He kissed my damp cheeks. "Will you let me do that? My love?"

"You are maddening. Because I love you so much, yes, you can do that." I leaned against him and let a few tears fall. He'd bought me a Chanel suit. Damnable, sweet, almost perfect man. Yes, I'd have to keep an eye on him. He'd want to take over my life. But there were worse things he could do. I felt that nagging fear shift inside me. My mother was out there. Plotting. And her idea of taking over my life wasn't out of generosity but because she wanted to manipulate me. No, I couldn't think about her now. Couldn't let her ruin this perfect moment.

"Thank you, Gloriana. I know that wasn't easy for you." Jerry kissed me then, sweetly, then with a hunger that was never far below the surface. When he pulled back we were both aroused, our minds on one thing.

"Jerry…" I pushed my fingers into his hair.

"No. Not yet. Aren't you eager to try on the suit?" He picked it up and handed it to me.

"That can wait." I was more interested in taking off clothes than putting them on. I had pulled open all the buttons on his navy shirt and now ran my fingers over the hard planes of his chest.

He shook his head. "No, I want to see you in it. Why don't you go into the bathroom, slip it on and then let me come in and take it off of you? Shall we make that bathroom our first room to celebrate Christmas properly in?" Jerry's grin had turned wicked.

"Sounds like a plan." I slid off his lap with a wiggle that made him groan then gathered up his gift. My gift to him? Me, of course. And he could bite me wherever he pleased.

Take a sneak peek at the next book from

GERRY BARTLETT

*R*eal *V*ampires
Say Read My Hips

ONE

Lacy attacked me when I walked into the shop. "Let me see that ring again. Oh my God, it's huge!" She held my hand, her grin wide. "Are you ready for the wedding yet?"

"New Year's Day is way too soon. Of course not." I felt like I was on a runaway train when Lacy squealed and started ranting about details that I hadn't even considered.

"I know. But Jerry's determined to get the knot tied before I change my mind." I sank down on the stool we kept for customers near the cash register. "Wow. Do you realize we've never even lived together for any length of time? At least not since we first met." I leaned closer. "And that was hundreds of years ago." I'd resisted that eternal commitment for over four hundred years.

So what had changed? Me. I was finally ready to admit that he was the one. Oh, let me say that again. THE ONE. After centuries of struggling against his domineering warrior nature and worrying that he'd never let me be independent, I'd finally realized we'd worked out a relationship I could live with. Actually, he'd changed too. Miracles do happen.

"Are you insane?" My mother suddenly appeared in the middle of the dress section. Yes, just materialized.

"Mother!" I glanced around, afraid some unsuspecting customer had fainted from shock.

"Give me some credit, Gloriana. None of your mortal customers saw me. Though I am sorely tempted to nip into the dressing room and tell the woman in there that she'll never get her butt into that size ten." My mother is a goddess from Olympus. She has a giant ego and considers mere mortals insignificant. I knew there was little chance she'd bother.

"You will not." I grabbed her arm and dragged her toward the back of the store. "Spandex can do wonders. If she wants to fit into a ten, I'm sure she'll manage it." I waved at Lacy to check. Zippers in the vintage clothes we sell in my shop weren't so forgiving.

"Oh, good. We're going to your back room. We need to have a mother-daughter talk." She was now the one doing the dragging, her fingers clamped on my arm. I gave Lacy a "save me" look but my were-cat manager had already found a size twelve and was halfway to the dressing room. Lacy has a bossy mother too. She did give me a sympathetic finger wave.

When the door finally closed behind me, I jerked my arm free. "I hope you're not here to disturb my wedding, Mother. You have to know I love Jerry. Why wouldn't I eventually marry him?"

"Because you have good sense, of course. He's a vampire, Gloriana." My mother shuddered. She sat in my only chair and crossed her legs. This season's Prada pumps in black lizard. Gorgeous. She always had on the most exquisite clothes. She materialized them with goddess magic which I envied.

"Don't say vampire like it's a bad word. You know what I am, Mother. That makes Jerry and me perfect for each other." I sat on my work table. "It took me a long time to realize it, but I'm ready to commit."

"Commit to an asylum perhaps. We have those on Olympus, darling. They're hell-holes. You should hear the screams. When a god or goddess goes off the deep end, the poor dears throw lightning bolts at anyone and everyone. It's quite annoying." My mother glanced at my concrete floor then kept her Gucci bag in her lap. "Obviously they must be locked away until they come to their senses. The screams are from the handmaidens who must care for them. The gods are stuck in tiny little cells, something like the coffins I've heard your council uses for punishment." Another delicate shudder.

"You sound like you've been there yourself,

Mother. I hope this isn't a hint that mental illness runs in the family." I saw that I'd struck a nerve. Mean, maybe, but I was tired of her attitude. She hated what I was so naturally that meant Jerry was worthless too. "Luckily I've never actually seen the coffins. They're for vampires who break council law. I try to follow the rules here."

"I never said I had to be locked up. But I've visited friends there. I know you're angry with me, Gloriana, but please try to understand. It takes a lot to make a god go insane but I've seen it happen. Because Zeus drove the person to madness." She glared at me with eyes the same blue as mine. Hers shot sparks which was pretty and scary at the same time. "He can do that when he's angry. I'm afraid that when he discovers I've lied to him because I kept you a secret all these years, he'll let me have it." She lowered her head and sniffed. "I'm not sure I can handle his worst when he throws it at me."

"Then your best move is to disavow me, Mother. Write me off. Head back to Olympus as if I never existed." I hopped down to kneel in front of her when tears filled her eyes. "Don't get me wrong. It's been wonderful finding out I have a family after all this time and I'd hate to lose you. I've been so... alone in the world. Except for Jerry." I took a breath.

"Darling. We *are* family. You and me, even Zeus." My mother dabbed at her eyes with a hanky she pulled from her purse. "What you feel for that vampire is gratitude. Even *I* am grateful to him. For saving you and keeping you alive for me."

"He certainly didn't do it for you, Mother." I stood and looked down at her. "He loves me. For over four hundred years, he's taken care of me and always been there for me. Now I'm finally strong enough to commit to him. Before . . ." I looked away from her. "Well, I was insecure. Afraid to use my powers. Not sure I even knew what they were."

"And now?" Her hand was on my shoulder.

"Now I know who I am and what I'm capable of." I turned to face her again and took her hand. "Thank you for that. So I'm confident that I can hold my own with Jerry, as an equal."

"Well, at least you're giving me credit for something." She took a breath. "I blame Achelous for all of this vampire madness." She frowned. "He will pay for tossing you away and forgetting you."

"Well, I hope so. But remember who left me with him in the first place. You lost the right to tell me what to do when you abandoned me in his orphanage, Mother. So accept my decision gracefully, please. I'm marrying Jerry and that's that." I put as much distance between us as the small room allowed and waited to see what she'd do. Toss a lightning bolt? It was one of her favorite tricks. It wasn't smart to stay too close to any of the gods or goddess from Olympus when they were pissed.

"Well." She stared at me, obviously thinking about her next move. "Am I invited to this event? Will there be bridal showers? A rehearsal dinner?" She pulled out a cell phone.

I could only gawk. I had no idea she even owned one. "Of course. Jer and I have many friends. In fact, Flo is hosting a bridesmaid dinner for me tomorrow night."

She punched something into her phone. "Surely you were going to have your mother there. What would your friends think if I didn't come? And I will bring an appropriate gift. Is there a theme?"

"I, uh, you know Flo, or maybe you don't. Anyway, she's having it at her house. It's lovely. I'll text you directions if you'll give me your number." I heard my own phone, which I kept in my pants pocket, chime.

"There, you have it." She smiled as if we were just the most ordinary bride and her adoring mother. "The theme, Gloriana. And are you registered anywhere?"

I swallowed, not sure this wasn't a ploy of some kind. "Seriously? You're going to come to Flo's party and act like a happy mother of the bride? You won't cause a scene? Throw lightning bolts? Burn her beautiful house down?"

"Well, clearly you don't trust me." Her hand trembled where it held her phone. "I am trying to understand you, Gloriana. You say you love and are grateful to this vampire. You wish to marry him. I want to have a relationship with you so I must not stand in the way of your happiness. Correct?" She moistened her lips with her tongue, as if she were nervous.

"Yes. Thank you, Mother." I hugged her then stepped back again, still not sure this wasn't all for show. "Flo is doing an Arabian nights theme. She wants us to come dressed in harem clothes. She does love costumes. And my shop has plenty of that kind of garb. Leave it to Flo to think of something that will stimulate my business."

"Why, it sounds like fun. I knew Scheherazade. Such a clever girl. And she loved beautiful clothes. I may have something I can conjure that will be perfect." She clapped her hands, suddenly all smiles.

"Flo promises some surprises. I'll text you where I'm registered. Don't know why, but Flo insisted Jer and I sign up for all the typical newlywed things."

"You are setting up housekeeping, aren't you? It is only proper." She tapped her foot. "I have much to do. A mother of the bride dress. I never thought I'd need such a thing. What are your colors?"

"I'm wearing red, Flo is wearing whatever she wants. We haven't--"

"Oh, dear. You clearly needed a wedding planner. But I suppose it's too late for that." She looked me over. "Yes, red's a good color for you. And lucky, I think. I will ask my astrologer about the date too. You did say New Year's Day. Hmm." Her brow wrinkled. "The party is tomorrow? That doesn't leave me much time. Text me when it starts. I wouldn't want to be late." She brushed my cheek with a light kiss. "I'd better go."

"About Zeus." Probably stupid to bring it up, but I knew she hadn't forgotten about taking me to Olympus. "Seriously. He doesn't need to know I even exist."

"Nonsense. My father will see you and love you on sight. I know it. You are the very image of my mother. That will soften him to me and make him forget my little fabrications." She managed a tremulous smile. "You mustn't worry about that."

"I think hiding an affair with a mortal and the resulting child for more than a thousand years is more than a *little* fabrication." I really, really didn't want to go to Olympus. "And what about the fact that I'm a vampire? How is Zeus going to take that?"

My mother actually bit her fingernail, a sign she was highly disturbed. When she realized she'd chipped her red polish, she frowned and blinked to fix it.

"Oh, he can never know that." She sighed and pasted on a smile. "Trust me to spin this situation to our advantage when the time comes. Now I'm off to check my closet. Mother of the bride. I simply cannot wrap my head around it." She dropped her cell into her bag and then disappeared.

I was still trying to process my mother's surprising change in attitude when the door into the storeroom was flung open. My best friend ran inside to wrap me in a hug. "Glory! Lacy called me and said your mother is here and causing trouble. As Matron of Honor I am ready to protect you. Where is she? Do I have to send her skinny butt straight back to where she came from?" Florence da Vinci held me against her soft bosom.

The idea of my little friend taking on my mother was so ridiculous that I laughed. But once I started, I couldn't stop. Oh, God. My mother's sudden determination to get involved in my wedding plans scared the hell out of me.

"*Amica*! What did she say? What did she do?"

"You won't believe it. She's all over the wedding now. She's coming to your party and is looking for a Mother of the Bride dress as we speak." I leaned back and wiped my eyes. "But thanks for the hug, Flo, I needed it."

"Did she do her usual vampire bashing?" Flo sat in the same chair my mother had just vacated. My friend also had on expensive shoes and a designer dress. It reminded me of my new goal—to make a big success of my business so I could afford to buy my own high end clothes. Flo might be content to take things from her rich husband, but I was fighting against the urge to just relax and let Jerry turn me into his trophy wife.

"She started in on it, but I shut her down. I'm not going to listen to her disrespect Jerry. I think she got the message." My phone chimed and I pulled it out of my pocket. "She just texted me. I'm supposed to send her the list of where I'm registered. It's been less than five minutes and she's bugging me already." I began to punch in the answers. "Let me send it now so she'll leave me alone."

"*Mio Dio*. Hebe at the party." Flo fanned her face with her hand. "I must order in more blood with alcohol. We'll both need it, eh?"

I hit send then grinned at Flo. "Definitely." I walked over to a rack and pulled out my costume for tomorrow night. "What do you think? Is this too much?" The crop top dipped low in front and was covered in gold sequins. Low riding harem pants in emerald green were made of a sheer fabric that was gathered and full, though there were bands of the gold at the waist and the ankles.

"It's perfect!" Flo jumped up to examine the fabric. "When Jeremiah sees you in this, he will carry you off to the bedroom so fast, you won't have time to open even one present. Better hide it from him until after the party."

I grinned and held it against me. "It is pretty bold. I've got some gold lame bikini panties to wear under it but that's all. He will love it."

"I have an outfit in red. Similar but with a bra top and a cute little jacket. I hope you are selling plenty of costumes here in your shop for this party. Are you?" Flo sat again.

"Yes, thanks to you and your clever theme, Flo. I know some people will expect me to just marry Jerry and give up this place, but I want to make it even bigger and better."

Flo shook her head, clearly mystified. "Of course you've always had this thing about independence. *Sciocchezza*, if you ask me." Flo opened her purse, a vintage piece that made me want to snatch it up and stick a price tag on it. "You marry a rich man, *amica*, so you should enjoy letting him take care of you."

"Did you just call me crazy?" I knew we didn't have the same philosophy when it came to men but I hoped we weren't going to fight about it.

"No, no. Just a little foolish." She smiled.

"Jerry understands that I like to make my own money. He's even going to help me with a business plan."

"Well. I am surprised." Flo glanced at my new tablet and the pile of bills next to it. "He has always struck me as a very, um, how you say, traditional man. He likes to travel, check on his other investments. Don't you think he will want you with him on those trips once you're married?"

"We'll work it out." Though my stomach had gone into free fall. Trust Flo to zero in on my main worry. Jerry had always been traditional, a polite way to say he was a throwback to his sixteenth century Highland roots. Little woman in the castle bedroom. That's where he'd like me to stay. At least vampire women weren't expected to cook, but he'd like nothing more than for me to fetch him a drink—if he hadn't preferred human donors.

Flo frowned. "I have said too much. Now you are worrying. I shut up and go. Come early tomorrow night. Help me with your mother. I don't trust her. Do you?"

"Not at all. She gave up too easily on her plan to take me off to Olympus and introduce me to my grandfather Zeus. Of course she's still plotting." I hugged Flo tight. "Together we will handle whatever trouble she starts."

"Of course!" She patted my back. "I'm just glad you finally said yes to Jeremiah. He's been very patient with you."

"Yes, he has. I'm lucky he didn't find another woman." I remembered a real bitch from his past we'd managed to run out of town not long ago. "Or at least the *right* other woman."

"He's yours now. And I sense he's coming. I go out the back." Flo winked. "Take care of him. Do not be too stubborn about some things." She looked around the back room again and gestured at that stack of bills. "Are you really so crazy about this little shop? Jeremiah is a wealthy man. Enjoy what he can give you. We could go shopping together, in Paris, Roma. I have wished for this a long time. Don't be stubborn, Glory. Let him take care of you as he has always wanted to do."

I refused to fight with my best friend. She just didn't understand how different we were. She rushed out the back door just as the one from the shop opened again and Jerry walked in, his smile taking my breath away. I had never seen him happier. I ran up to him and threw my arms around him.

"That's a fine welcome." He leaned down and took my mouth with his. There it was, the perfect kiss that reassured me we were meant to be. I savored his taste, the way we fit. I sighed when he pulled back.

We were both smiling and I saw that he was flushed. Of course I hadn't done *that*. He'd obviously found a blood donor in an alley along busy Sixth Street on his way to meet me.

"I'm glad to see you. Flo just left. We were talking about the bridal party. I have a sexy costume to wear. What do you think about the Arabian Nights?" I twined my fingers through his curls. He had let his hair grow almost to his shoulders and it was a look I loved.

"If you're going to be my harem of one, I'm eager to try an Arabian night." He glanced at the rack where my costume was hanging. "Is yours the green number that I can see through? Try it on now and give me a preview." He slid a hand down to my hip to pull me closer.

"Mmm. Tempting, but no." I leaned against him. Flo had raised questions I wanted answered. "Can we talk?"

"If we must." He let me go and sat on the table, patting the space beside him. "What's on your mind? Lacy said your mother was here earlier. Did she upset you?"

"She tried. When that didn't work, she decided to get on the wedding bandwagon. I'm still not sure I believe her act, but she says she's coming to the wedding and all the other festivities." I sat and leaned against him. He was so solid, so reliably mine. I slid my arm around his waist. "But forget her. Flo made me think about our future."

"What about it?" He stiffened under my fingertips. "Damn it, Gloriana, I will not take that ring back."

"I'm not changing my mind, just trying to work

out logistics." I felt him relax again. I'd made my big strong Highlander insecure about our relationship with my hot and cold attitude and my affair with another man. He'd forgiven but he hadn't forgotten. I was going to have to work to make him trust me not to back out of this commitment.

"Logistics. We've settled the living arrangements, of course." He kissed my nose.

"Yes, I love our new apartment." I'd been surprised when Jerry had bought the apartment building that also housed my shop. Then he'd evicted the other tenants on the second floor so we could have a large apartment. At first I'd seen his taking over the living arrangements as high-handed and manipulative. I'd finally realized that was my kneejerk reaction to almost everything he did when he was simply trying to please me. It wasn't easy for me to accept gifts from Jerry, but I was learning to do it.

"This is turning out to be a good investment. If you ever decide to give up the shop, this space could easily be rented out to someone else. Places on Sixth Street are always in demand. The rents from the apartments upstairs along with the shops down here, including yours and Mugs and Muffins next door, bring in a good income." He set a folder on the table next to him.

"I don't plan to give up the shop." I ignored his hands on my back as he pulled me closer. "You aren't counting on that, are you?"

"Don't get your panties in a twist, Gloriana. I wasn't suggesting such a thing." He smiled and traced my frown line which I knew had appeared between my brows. "In fact, I have a wedding present for you." He reached for the folder and put it in my hands. "Look and see."

"What is it?" I flipped it open, then gasped. "Jerry! It's the deed to this building. You, you put it in my name." I scanned the document. There was a lot of legalese but the meaning was clear. Jeremy Blade, the name he was going by in Austin, had deeded this property over to one Gloriana St. Clair for the sum of one dollar.

"No, I sold it to you. You owe me a dollar. I figure you're good for it." He was grinning, entirely pleased with himself.

"This is too much!" I blinked as tears filled my eyes. I'd never owned a piece of property in my life. And I had a feeling the price Jer had paid Damian just a month ago had been in the seven figures.

"Nothing is too much for you, my love." He rubbed a tear off my cheek. "Did I surprise you?"

"Surprise? You've blown me away. I don't know what to say." I looked the deed over again. It was real. I owned this entire block. On Austin's Sixth Street. I worried for a minute, thinking about taxes and insurance, then deliberately put all that out of my mind. Jerry said the income was good. It would cover such things. And, if I couldn't afford it, I could always sell it.

"You're awfully quiet. *Is* it too much?" He was starting to look worried. "You know I'd give you much more if you'd let me."

"So you've said." I sighed and carefully set the folder on the table next to him. "I was thinking how much I like it here."

"True. We've both lived many places. Austin seems like home, doesn't it?" Jerry pulled me close. "Someday we'll have to move, but not anytime soon."

"No, not anytime soon." I leaned against him. "I'll always remember Austin now. Where we made our home. Where we married. We have such good friends here."

"That we do." He ran a thumb across my cheek and to the back of my neck so that our lips almost touched. "You've built a fine business here. I admire that. Keep it as long as you wish. I'll help any way I can. Or leave you to it. Just tell me what you want, my love. Owning the building will give you options. You can expand if you wish. Kick out the tattoo parlor next door if you need that space." He didn't have to pull me close this time as I kissed him with all the love that I had. When I finally leaned back, I rested my head against his shoulder..

"Have I told you how much I love you, Jeremiah Campbell?" I ran my hand over his chest, loving the hard contours of my warrior.

"I never get tired of hearing it, lass." He lifted my chin and kissed me, lying back on the table, until I was stretched out on top of him.

"Wait!" I wrenched out of his arms and rescued my computer, bills and that precious deed, stowing them on a shelf before I ripped off my sweater to fling it across the room. Then I locked the doors.

"Is this *my* wedding present?" He grinned up at me as he reached for the front clasp of my skimpy black lace bra.

"Well, since I can't afford buildings, I guess this will have to do. How can you keep surprising me?" I unbuttoned his cotton shirt so I could smooth my hands over his chest. Bending over him, I licked my way from one nipple to the other, sucking one into my mouth.

"I consider it a constant challenge." He moaned when I dragged a fang along his skin, drawing blood then licking it away.

"Good. I want to keep you on your toes, lover." This man was mine and I wasn't going to let him forget it.

"Gloriana." He groaned and pushed his hands into the back of my jeans. Got to love spandex. I wasn't about to admit the size of mine. In fact, I cut out the tag as soon as I got them. Some things Jerry just didn't need to know.

I sat up and opened my jeans then hopped off the table to wrestle them off. I didn't want to delay things while Jerry tried to pry them off. He'd been busy getting naked himself and kicked his own jeans away then lifted me to the edge of the table where he stood between my legs. He kissed me endlessly while his fingers worked their magic. I ran my hands over his hard body, finding all the places I knew made him groan with pleasure. There's a lot to be said for centuries of history together. The miracle was that we had never tired of each other. That the spark not only still glowed but burst into bright flames at every touch.

He ran his tongue around each of my nipples, his fangs nipping and playing until I pulled on his hair, moaning with pleasure. Then he sank to his knees, breathing in my scent before he pressed his mouth between my thighs. I grasped his ears. There was no need to guide him since he knew just how to make me shriek my release. So soon. I crossed my feet behind his head, rocking into him as he found and plucked the sensitive nub with his lips. My hips arched off that hard table as excitement shivered through me. I was close again. But I wouldn't let him make me come without him. Not this time.

"God, Jerry! I need you inside me! Now." I actually remembered that the door into the shop wasn't soundproof. Of course the clerks out there were paranormals who could hear things mortals couldn't. Still... The music in the shop got louder. I collapsed back on the table, pulling Jerry up until his erection teased me, nudging for entrance. But he wouldn't give me what I wanted. Not yet.

"Say it again, Gloriana. Say you'll marry me on New Year's Day. Nothing will stop us from becoming man and wife. Nothing." He was serious, his muscular arms bulging as he held himself just above me. His face was inches from mine, his eyes dark and serious.

"I love you, Jeremiah Campbell, Jeremy Blade, any name you call yourself. I'll always be yours. Only yours. And on the first day of the New Year, I'll declare it before all of our friends. Now take me before I go mad." I scored his back with my nails, afraid I was about to do something mean with my Olympus powers if he didn't put me out of my misery.

"I love you, Gloriana. And I'm never letting you go." He plunged into me then, the pressure of his cock all it took to make me bite back my scream of release. I shuddered, feeling my completion rocket through me. His mouth on mine swallowed my squeal of pleasure. I pounded on his back, my heels sliding up and down the backs of his strong legs.

But Jerry wasn't finished, not by a long shot. He kept staring into my eyes--trying to read my mind? I wasn't about to let him. I could block my thoughts and did. He was never letting me go? Fine. That worked both ways. I wanted to belong to him now. He was as tied to me as I was to him. Marriage. In the vampire world it was even more difficult to break that bond than it was for mortals. We were a fairly small community and it was inevitable that we'd see each other, run into each other. Only death would part us. And death for a vampire was rare and never natural.

He held my hips and began a slow seduction again. Teasing me, he kept pulling out until I begged him to push deeper, go faster. He stayed in control, his face solemn until I saw him finally lose it. He began to drive into me, finding the perfect angle that he knew would send me over the brink again. Yes, the tension was there, building, tightening inside me until my toes curled. For a moment I resisted. I didn't want... But this was Jerry, my beloved, the man who would do anything for me. Even buy me a damned building.

My second orgasm broke me into a thousand pieces as Jerry shouted his own release. I let him go, my hands landing on the wooden table. He lay on me for a few moments, his lips brushing my throat gently. It was a sweet vampire kiss showing love, not hunger for my blood.

When he finally rolled off of me with a satisfied groan I opened my eyes to stare at the cheap acoustical tiles above my head. I realized my hands were fisted and I opened them finger by finger then ran my hand over his hair-roughened stomach and felt the muscles contract. I loved how masculine he was. I did. I loved *him*.

Jerry's heavy hand landed on my thigh, like he owned it. I turned my head and saw his smile.

Satisfaction. Happiness. Not possession. He was glad we'd be together forever. I managed my own smile. If I had doubts I would chalk them up to bridal nerves. Yes, that had to be it. Everything Jerry did for me was out of love, not for any other reason.

"I have an appointment with my lawyer for you to sign that deed in front of a notary, Gloriana. A formality. That will make it yours. Can you come with me now?" Jerry jumped off the table, eager to get to business. He grabbed his jeans and stepped into them.

I wasn't about to lie around naked and exposed under those fluorescent lights. I was right behind him, snapping on my bra, pulling my sweater over my head. I'd just stepped into my panties when he held my jeans just out of reach.

"You're awfully quiet, Gloriana. Is this a bad time?" He was serious, watching me.

I grabbed a belt loop and tugged him close then kissed his lips, wishing he'd smile again. I could see that he wanted to please me and I was going to have to stop imagining control issues that just weren't there.

"You can't know how much I love that you're doing this for me. It's perfect." I slid my hands down his chest then around his waist. "This marriage should be a partnership, Jerry. How can I ever match this kind of generosity?"

"Don't be ridiculous." He jerked me closer. "All I've wanted for centuries is to make you happy." He dropped the jeans and slid his hands down to cup my butt. "You want to give me something? Give me two weeks away from this shop. For a proper honeymoon. Can the girls handle that?" His smile was back, a wicked one this time that promised all kinds of naughty honeymoon delights.

"Hmm. Sure." I ran my fingers through his thick hair. "Where will we go?" Sandy beaches and moonlight. Or maybe a mountain chalet. Someplace far away from Austin and my stupid doubts.

"Anywhere you wish." He kissed me one more time then stepped back. "Now are you coming with me to the lawyer's office?"

"Can you give me half an hour? Lacy needs to take a dinner break then I can meet you there."

"Perfect." He kissed me, pressed the card with the address into my hand then slipped out the back door. I sat in my own chair for a change and realized I probably had a goofy grin on my face. I was beginning to think this was going to work. We could be happy. He was respecting me. My doubts were silly. I struggled into my jeans then just sat there, finally sure I could go through with it. I was going to marry Jeremiah Campbell and have an amazing honeymoon.

"I can see that I will have to take drastic measures."

"Mother? You weren't spying on me, were you?"

"Unfortunately." She was back and glaring at me from beside the back door. "It is not something that I enjoy. Bacchanals in Rome were more entertaining."

"That's disgusting." I was sure my face was as red as her Gucci handbag. "What do you mean by drastic measures?"

"I'm sorry that I have to do this, but you leave me no choice, Gloriana." She raised her hand.

I blinked and the crowded back room in my shop was gone. Instead I was lying on a bed. It was a golden monstrosity and huge, an ornate four poster.

The canopy over my head was draped with gold and white silk. Under me I could feel more silk and big fluffy pillows. I struggled to sit up and look around. The bedroom had fancy French furniture, clearly vintage and that must have cost a fortune. Looking down I saw one of those gorgeous rugs that would feel like velvet under my feet. I was still dressed in my jeans and sweater though my feet were bare. My shoes were on the floor next to the bed. Where the hell was I?

"Mother? What have you done?"

"What you forced me to do, daughter." She appeared next to me. There was a woman behind her. A woman in a toga. Oh, God. "Here, enjoy your first meal. I'm sure you've been craving chocolate. And how about some croissants? You won't believe what they do with pastry here." She flicked her wrist and the woman set the tray down on my lap.

My eyes watered as the aroma of fresh hot chocolate wafted from a delicate bone china cup. Next to it sat a pair of flaky pastries and a bowl of glistening strawberry preserves. All of it was laid out to perfection on a tray set with a linen napkin and sterling silver flatware.

"What the hell is this? Are you into torturing me now? You know I can't eat."

"Yes, you can. Here." My mother smiled. "Welcome to Olympus, darling."

Coming in fall 2014.
Order online and in
bookstores everywhere.

ABOUT THE AUTHOR

Gerry Bartlett is a native Texan and lives halfway between Houston and Galveston. When she's not writing her bestselling *Real Vampires* series, she is treasure hunting for her antiques business on the historic Strand in Galveston. You can read more about Gerry and her series at gerrybartlett.com, friend her on Facebook, follow her on twitter @gerrybartlett or Instagram.

CPSIA information can be obtained
at www.ICGtesting.com
Printed in the USA
LVOW13s1006190117
521517LV00015B/236/P